THE DETERMINED MISTRESS

The De Petras Saga, Book 4

Emily E K Murdoch

ARE YOU SIGNED UP FOR DRAGONBLADE'S BLOG?

You'll get the latest news and information on exclusive giveaways, exclusive excerpts, coming releases, sales, free books, cover reveals and more.

Check out our complete list of authors, too!

No spam, no junk. That's a promise!

Sign Up Here

www.dragonbladepublishing.com

Dearest Reader;

Thank you for your support of a small press. At Dragonblade Publishing, we strive to bring you the highest quality Historical Romance from some of the best authors in the business. Without your support, there is no 'us', so we sincerely hope you adore these stories and find some new favorite authors along the way.

Happy Reading!

CEO, Dragonblade Publishing

Additional Dragonblade books by Author Emily E K Murdoch

The De Petras Saga
The Misplaced Husband (Book 1)
The Impoverished Dowry (Book 2)
The Contrary Debutante (Book 3)
The Determined Mistress (Book 4)
The Convenient Engagement (Book 5)

The Governess Bureau Series
A Governess of Great Talents (Book 1)
A Governess of Discretion (Book 2)
A Governess of Many Languages (Book 3)
A Governess of Prodigious Skill (Book 4)
A Governess of Unusual Experience (Book 5)
A Governess of Wise Years (Book 6)

Never The Bride Series
Always the Bridesmaid (Book 1)
Always the Chaperone (Book 2)
Always the Courtesan (Book 3)
Always the Best Friend (Book 4)
Always the Wallflower (Book 5)
Always the Bluestocking (Book 6)
Always the Rival (Book 7)
Always the Matchmaker (Book 8)
Always the Widow (Book 9)
Always the Rebel (Book 10)
Always the Mistress (Book 11)
Always the Second Choice (Book 12)
Always the Mistletoe (Novella)
Always the Reverend (Novella)

CHAPTER ONE

September 3, 1812

"I S SHE NOT the most precious thing you ever—"

"More precious than Beryl?"

"Oh, comparing babies is a fool's game!"

Micah de Petras sighed heavily. It was not as though he had expected to be the center of attention; with three sisters, one learned quickly where the focus of the room always laid.

But still. He had been invited to his parents' home to share the news of his latest win on the horses. Wasn't that what his father had said?

Yet, there they were, gathered by Coral, as though no one had ever had a baby before.

Micah leaned back in his armchair, glass of port in hand, and wondered just how long it would take before they realized he was gone, if he slipped out through the parlor door.

A minute? An hour?

The baby in his sister's arms blew a raspberry, and the entire room sighed.

"I never thought I could love something quite so much," said Coral with a weary smile. "Except Edward, of course!"

Her husband smiled. "Don't you worry, I love her far more than I ever loved you."

The family chuckled as Micah rolled his eyes. *Really.* Edward was all very well as a brother-in-law, and as a Duke, he had been remarkably useful, as giving the man's name to his creditors always permitted an extension.

But the tripe the man came up with! His eldest sister, Coral, had never been a gushing sort of woman, but since the baby arrived…

"She is so precious," said Amethyst, cooing over the baby. "Why, I—"

"Careful," said Coral sternly, leaning away with the babe in her arms. "Do not get too close."

Micah watched with interest as his cousin flushed at his sister's words. Women. They could make something complicated even if there was nothing there to complicate.

"She is so darling—"

"I know quite what you mean," said Emerald quietly.

Micah glanced over at the middle sister of his family. Emerald, shy, quiet, hardly able to give an opinion without feeling embarrassed by it, flushed as the room turned to her.

"I just meant—well, when baby Beryl—"

"I still don't know how you managed to name her that," groaned her husband.

Micah snorted. "You think any men in this family get a say, Swindmore?"

The Marquess of Swindmore grinned. "Oh, I knew the de Petras women got their own way long before I married one."

"Robert!"

Micah sighed at his sister Emerald's words.

That was the problem with sisters, wasn't it? He had no fault to lay against them as people he supposed; they were relatively harmless. In fact, on some occasions, he would even go so far as to say that he liked his sisters.

Coral was sharp and direct, which he liked, even if she was a little snooty at times. Becoming a duchess, it appeared, would do that to you. They never agreed, but that was beside the point.

Emerald, shy and nervous, never got in the way yet had a spark in her for the things that really mattered that Micah had to admire, even if he rarely saw it.

And as for Sapphire…

"Well, I think all babies look the same at this age," announced the youngest de Petras, dark hair flying as she strode across the room to peer at the baby. "Look at her, all light hair and big blue eyes. I honestly couldn't tell any difference between Amber and Beryl. We'll have to wait and see who she takes after."

"Her mother, I hope," said her father with a grin.

"Oh, I imagine she'll be a bit of both," said Opal de Petras comfortably from her armchair by the fire.

Micah shot his mother a glance. Opal appeared very pleased with herself, or at least, the state of affairs, and why wouldn't she? All four of her children under one roof, along with their cousin—a rarity, his own fault, he knew.

Spending time with his family…well, it was not something Micah sought out. In truth, it was something he avoided. It was never long before the conversation ended up returning to—

"Well, now baby Amber is here, safe and sound," said Opal smartly, "there are no more family celebrations. Unless Micah has a secret engagement he would like to share?"

Micah groaned.

And there it was. How long was that—ten minutes after he had stepped foot into the place? And they wondered why he had taken lodgings, even though they all lived in London!

"Opal," said her husband in a low, warning tone.

Micah glanced at his father with a look of gratitude, but it appeared Jasper did not recognize it as such. He frowned back at his son, and Micah looked away immediately.

Well, he should not have expected any support from that quarter, he supposed. It was all very well hoping that the men of the family could stick together, but then, they were not a normal family, were they?

"What?" asked Opal, a picture of innocence. "I only asked—"

"You know how Micah feels about marriage, Mama," said Sapphire with a snorting laugh. "Anyone would think you're attempting to chase him out of here!"

"Sapphy!"

"What?" asked Sapphire with a wicked grin.

Both of her parents frowned as the youngest de Petras giggled, walking to sit by the window. "I do not see why I should not say it, so many gentlemen do."

"No gentlemen you know of, I am sure," said Coral reprovingly.

Micah rolled his eyes. Trust Coral to get involved. *Just because she was the heir—*

"James says it," Sapphire said innocently.

"Well, the Earl of Maltravers should know better than to speak in such a way before a young lady!" said Opal tartly. "Really, I had expected better of that young man. We've known him all his life, and—"

"Maltravers is almost part of the family," Jasper reminded her. "I suppose he does not think of Sapphire as a young lady."

Micah snorted. Sapphire shot him a glare, but he merely stuck his tongue out, and a smile slipped on her lips.

"Well, I hardly think him a suitable friend for a lady seeking matrimony…"

It was easy to ignore what his mother was saying, Micah mused. He had first noticed it a few years ago when Coral had married. Then it was his turn—at least, supposedly. He was the next eldest child, but so far he had managed to avoid anything so odious as marriage.

"—in Society a year or two now, and would benefit from a wider pool of introductions to gentlemen—and with Amethyst now with us…"

Micah watched as Coral offered her unsolicited opinion on whatever it was they were talking about—of course she did—and Emerald merely sat and allowed the conversation to wash over her, too.

He caught her eye, and she colored slightly, though goodness knew why. He had never met a woman so…so uncomfortable in company, even the company of her own family. It was little wonder she and her husband lived just outside town in their own home far from the rush of people. It was a marvel she had even bothered to—

A clock chimed. Micah's attention was drawn to it immediately. Five o'clock.

That was the trouble when one's mother invited you over for afternoon tea. *Afternoon tea! Like he was some prim and proper lady of middling years!*

He had the awful habit of staying longer than intended, and if he stayed for much longer, Micah ran the risk of being invited to dine. Lord, he could end up spending the entire evening here—and that would mean not seeing…

A warm sort of ache settled in Micah's stomach.

Catherine Tetlow.

It was a Thursday, of course, and that meant Catherine. His favorite mistress, though in truth, he only had her and Polly on the books at the moment. Little Annie had gone off and got married, worse luck, and Bridget had been taken by her master up north.

That left Catherine.

Micah shifted in his seat. He was going to be late now. Their arrangement, every Thursday at six o'clock, had been longstanding and perfectly suited the two of them—but if he did not get a move on, he would never make it across Town in time.

Lord, to disappoint Catherine…

Micah smiled. She had a temper on her, that woman, and in a strange way, he did not like to disappoint her. There was something rather marvelous about a woman who knew what she wanted, when what she wanted was you.

"—don't you think, Micah?"

He blinked. The entire room's attention was on him again—worse luck.

"I beg your pardon?" he said lazily.

Coral rolled her eyes. "You never listen, Micah!"

"I listen to what interests me," he shot back. "Do not blame me if you never achieve those adulterated heights."

"You are—"

"We are speaking of your future marriage, Micah," cut in their mother.

Micah turned to glare at Opal. "There is no marriage to speak of, so the conversation will be of short duration."

"Just because you are not engaged to be married now does not mean you never will be," said Opal sharply. "Really, Micah, you speak as though matrimony were a disaster!"

"A prison," said Micah shortly.

They were pushing him to it. What else was he supposed to say? Lie and say every moment of every day he could not wait to be tied to one woman, one bed forever?

He shivered in his seat. *No, sir. Not for him.*

"A prison!"

He should have known it would be Coral who would be so offended.

"Prison is not precisely what I meant," added Micah hastily. *He should have made for the parlor door the moment everyone was crowded around the baby...* "I just meant—"

"Prison is certainly not what I would call it," said Opal hotly. "Would you, Jasper?"

"I wouldn't dare to have my own opinion, my dear," Jasper said with a wink.

Micah snorted as his father kissed his mother. *Honestly, did they have to be so—*

"Mama!"

"Papa, stop that!" said Sapphire with a giggle. "Poor old Edward and Robert don't know what to do with themselves!"

"Nor do I, if it comes to that!" spluttered Amethyst.

There was laughter throughout the room, and Micah's heart rose. Catherine would not mind, even if he was a few minutes late. Maybe even half an hour. If he could just creep out while everyone was—

"I just think you would be much happier with a wife," said Opal smartly, her attention once more turned to her son. "Micah—Micah, are you listening to me?"

"Wouldn't dare ignore you," he muttered.

"What was that?"

"I said yes, I am listening," Micah lied.

"Well, I am in no rush for Micah to get married," pronounced Sapphire from the window. "Just think, another woman joining the family! I rather think I would have to vet anyone who thought themselves brave enough to become a de Petras, don't you think?"

He had to smile. Sapphire's witty tongue and complete disregard for propriety made her, perhaps, the sibling most like himself, even with the nine-year age difference.

"They would certainly have to be brave," he said quietly.

"Foolish, more like," came the acerbic wit of Amethyst.

"And beautiful," said Opal with a dreamy smile. "And wealthy or well born."

"Or both," chimed in Jasper with a wink at Micah.

Micah did not return it. Why did his father think he could so easily slide into his good graces? Why, it was not as though his father ever defended him—truly defended him.

"Preferably someone we already know," said Coral, shifting the babe in her arms as it snuffled quietly. "It would be a lot easier if—"

"Is Miss Howarth still available?"

"Really, Mama!" Micah could not help himself, even though he had tried desperately not to get involved. "You cannot speak of ladies as though they were horses!"

"Miss Howarth announced her engagement a week ago," added Emerald quietly.

A dark flush tinged her cheeks as all looked at her in astonishment, including Micah.

Lizzie Howarth, engaged? To be married? It was unaccountable. No one would want to marry that woman, would they?

True, he had stolen more than a few kisses from the youngest Miss Howarth, and had once found himself rather awkwardly discovered with her pressed against him on a staircase...

But still. He had not expected anyone else to actually claim her.

Though Micah hated to admit it to himself, let alone anyone else, he found to his great surprise that he had rather counted on Miss Howarth as...well. A reserve. If his family kept on with these demands to wed, it was pleasant knowing there was a soppy, pretty girl who enjoyed receiving his kisses.

But engaged?

"Oh," said Opal, clearly as disappointed as Micah. "What a pity. I don't suppose there is any hope Lady Rose Romeril—"

"The day I find myself Lady Romeril's son-in-law would be a sad day indeed," interjected Micah with a dry laugh. "I know she is your friend, Mama, but—"

"Yes, I quite understand," said Opal eagerly, and there was an eager look in her eyes that Micah did not like.

Then he realized why. *Blast.* He had spoken, hadn't he, given an opinion as to the direction of his marriage. Now she was going to think—

"But I am glad you are considering these sorts of things, Micah," his mother said triumphantly. "I am sure it will help you secure a very suitable—"

"What does it matter anyway whether I marry or not?" Micah said heavily, knowing the words about to leave his mouth were unkind, cruel, and entirely true, but unable to stop himself anyway. "It does not matter whether I marry or not—I am not the heir! I'm not the one inheriting the family responsibility, Coral is!"

The words rang in the room as though they had been shot with a pistol.

Everyone acted differently, as Micah had known they would.

The two brothers-in-law, interlopers to the family, stepped to the side and spoke quietly together, evidently wishing to leave this awkward situation as soon as possible.

Amethyst looked between them, eyes wide, as though eager to understand precisely what was going on. Sapphire did nothing. Emerald flinched as though he had hurled an insult at her, which was nonsense as the whole thing had nothing to do with her, then glanced at…

Coral. Micah found himself almost a little afraid to look at his older sister.

Coral de Petras, Duchess of Glaenarm. She had not taken old Edward's surname when they had married, of course; that was the de Petras way.

Micah sighed heavily. *The de Petras way.* That was the trouble with being such an unusual family. They must be the only family in England to be headed by a woman, with a woman as the heir. And that left him…

Coral was looking proud, unblinkingly, accepting his anger and bitterness with far more calm than Micah thought was fair.

That was Coral all over. Never cowed, never backed into a corner. If she had been a man, Micah would have admitted she was a far better prospect for heading up the family once their parents were gone, God forbid it happen soon.

But she wasn't a brother. She was a sister, and Micah had had to bear the indignity of playing second fiddle to a sister ever since he had come of age. No wonder so many gentlemen of the *ton* mocked him.

"Really, Micah, that temper of yours," came the teasing refrain of Sapphire behind him. "It'll get you into trouble one day."

It was on the tip of his tongue for Micah to say it had already got him into trouble, and frequently, but he managed to bite down on the words.

That wouldn't help. His bitterness wouldn't help, his anger wouldn't help, and he could already see the disappointment in his father's gaze that he had managed to ruin, again, a family afternoon.

He must not let his temper get the better of him…which was all very well and good to think, but wasn't it already too late?

"It's never been something I have understood, actually," said Robert delicately.

Micah glanced at him, hoping beyond hope the man had a point and wasn't just saying something for the sake of filling the silence.

Robert cleared his throat. "Tell me—why do girls inherit in the de Petras family?"

Micah groaned. *Why did he have to open his—*

"It has always been that way," said Opal stiffly. "Coral will inherit."

"And that is why I will not," said Amethyst dryly. "Daughter of a son, not a daughter."

"Coral, and Amber after her," Opal said quietly.

Micah looked at the baby in his sister's arms. It was strange in a way, to think that until a few weeks ago, he could have been the second choice after Coral. But now this literal babe in arms superseded him. One day, when he was very old and very unfortunate, he could live to see both his mother and his older sister die…and that would leave this baby in charge of the de Petras family.

God forbid!

"Always been that way?" repeated Robert, a confused expression on his face. "But it must have started at some point."

Was that a frown on his mother's face? "As I said, it has always been that way—"

"And God forbid we do anything else," snapped Micah.

He had to leave this conversation, this family as soon as possible. She was waiting.

"Micah," came a quiet voice behind him.

He turned around to see Sapphire looking remarkably serious. It was so unlike her that, for a moment, he hardly knew what to say.

Then a smile slipped across his lips. "Do not come at me, little one."

Immediately, Sapphire's eyes flashed. "I am out in Society now, and have been for over a year, there is no need to call me—"

"I think it's time for me to go," said Micah shortly, rising to his feet.

He had expected to see relief in Coral's eyes, known it would be there the moment he announced he was leaving, but he had not expected it to hurt quite so much.

What had happened between them—when had it happened? Micah could hardly recall a time when he and Coral had not been at odds with each other. Did it always happen with the two eldest siblings, siblings with only months between them? Or was it something special between them? Had they managed to do what so many siblings had avoided, and find they did not each like each other that much?

"Oh, stay," said Opal hurriedly, rising to her own feet. "We do not have to talk about—and dinner will be announced soon—"

"I am sorry, Mama, I have a prior engagement," said Micah stiffly.

He nodded at the room at large, ignored pleas to stop, and strode into the hall.

Somehow it was cooler here. Had he really got himself into such a state that he was actually hot under the collar? Micah grabbed his greatcoat and had pulled one arm through a sleeve when a quiet voice behind him made him turn.

"Micah."

It was with a heavy sigh that Micah turned to look into the tired eyes of his father.

"I do not need a lecture, Papa," he said. "Please, just let me be on my way."

"You should not have spoken to your mother like that," said Jasper quietly.

There was no biting tone there, no anger,

just…disappointment. *Why was it*, Micah thought irritably as he pulled his other arm through its sleeve, *that disappointment was far worse to hear in one's parent than anger?* Dear God, it was like being a child again.

"I know," he said shortly.

"All she wants is—"

"What's best for me, I know," recited Micah. He almost knew his father's speech by heart now, there was so little variation. "And marriage has made you happy, Mama happy, Coral happy—even Emerald, and we all know how vociferously she denied it would."

There was a wistful smile on Jasper's face. "Just as you deny it."

Micah frowned. "Papa—"

"I just—being a part of this family is an honor, Micah," said Jasper quietly, as the gentle burble of conversation in the drawing room started up again, the door still ajar. "Many people would love to—"

"Well then, they can join," Micah interrupted, pushed beyond all endurance. *An honor?* His father had no idea what it was to be mocked wherever you went because you had no higher standing in your family than your sister—*your sister!* "It does not feel like an honor to be pushed aside, nor does it feel honorable to feel forced into marriage. I am sorry, Papa, but there it is. Enjoy your evening."

And without waiting for a response, Micah pulled open the door and stepped into the autumnal night.

CHAPTER TWO

Catherine Tetlow glared at the grandfather clock and tapped the glass. "Are you running fast?"

No one answered. *That was the problem with living on one's own,* Catherine thought wryly as she stared at the dial of numbers before her. She started to slip into habits that were altogether a little unsavory.

Like speaking to herself, for example.

The grandfather clock stared back, the same as it always had. When she had found it in an antique shop, desperate to furnish the two rooms she had taken in Parson's Buildings, she had rather liked the idea of having such a fine clock about the place. It would give her rooms—her *home*, she still struggled to think of this place as a home—an air of refinement.

Which was all very well, until the darned thing stopped working. Or was it working too well?

Catherine tapped the glass again. The clock hands pointed to a seven and a two, which simply could not be correct. Ten past seven in the evening? On a Thursday? And no Micah?

No, there must be a fault with the clock, though how she could go about fixing it, she had no idea. How much did it cost to have a clock mended these days?

Striding away from the irritating thing, Catherine sat heavily on the end of the striped chaise longue. Where was he?

Micah was never late. Sometimes he was early, desperate for her, eager to step into her embraces. Catherine shivered with a smile. He longed for her just as she longed for him, she was certain—had done since the moment they had first encountered each other.

Still. She was not so foolish as to think she was the only woman Micah de Petras was giving his affections to.

Catherine forced the thought from her mind. *She was not going to dwell on it.* She was not going to think of all the other women Micah was bedding. He paid her for a reason.

And she took his money for a reason. That was what she had to focus on, not her pique that she was not idealized or special in the eyes of a man who evidently did not know what was good for him.

That had to be good enough for her.

Rising, Catherine swept across the room she called her boudoir—at least, to Micah, who she had assumed would be impressed by such a thing—and fell gently onto the bed.

Honestly, if he was not going to arrive soon, she may as well—

A rattle at the door. Catherine sat up, heart racing, body tingling with anticipation for the arrival of—

Micah de Petras strode into the room, a glower on his face like she had never seen before. His hands were clenched, his greatcoat bundled up tight to his throat, and his eyes flashed as he slammed the door behind him.

"Catherine," he said.

Catherine's heart skipped a beat. How was it possible that just three syllables could have such an impact? She heard her name spoken all the time, but it never made her feel like this.

As though the whole world had stalled, centered for a few hours on her and Micah and nothing else.

"Micah de Petras," she said as lightly as she could manage. Did he hear the tremor in her voice? Did he have any idea how he made her feel? "I was beginning to think you weren't coming."

He snorted, pulling off his top hat and greatcoat and throwing them to the floor.

Catherine waited, knowing anything she said next could be wrong. That was always the way with Micah; his temper was hot and burned fast. The anger would be gone soon, and then they would embrace and kiss and—

"The cheek!" Micah exploded, gesturing at the door as though that would explain what he was talking about. "The very arrogance of telling me my own business, how my own life should go!"

Catherine rose from the bed, but she was not foolish enough to approach him. Not yet. "Your parents, again?"

"All of them!" spluttered Micah, anger still vivid on his face. "The way they talk to me as though I am incapable of making any decisions for myself. Only orders to obey!"

Catherine watched him, the frustration pouring from his lips as he spat it like poison.

She ached for him, ached to hold him, to kiss away the frustrations heaped upon him, but she waited. If she rushed in, if she tried to console him before he was ready…

Did anyone else know him as she did? Catherine smiled slightly but forced it away in case Micah misunderstood her and thought she was laughing at him. Surely there could not be anyone who understood him as she did.

Micah turned to look, fists unclenching as he stammered, "Y-You understand what I mean, don't you?"

And that was the signal. Catherine had heard this before, all of it. Oh, in different variations, on different days, about different arguments.

But it was all the same.

Micah de Petras wanted to be understood. And she understood. She could see every emotion dancing across his face, perhaps better than her own.

Catherine stepped forward, took those hands that had so recently been fisted, and kissed him lightly on the corner of his mouth. "I understand."

"They are completely impossible," Micah said. His voice was quieter now, calmer. His fingers tightened around hers. "Impossible."

"Hmm," Catherine murmured, nodding and kissing Micah on the other corner of his lips.

Those lips twitched. "Are you even listening to me, Catherine?"

"Would I dare to ignore you?" she teased, kissing just below his ear, and that was when she felt it, heard it.

Micah moaned. His shoulders loosened, and Catherine felt that rush when a person was close to you. Not just touching, not just kissing or bedding. Intimately woven together, your soul connected to their soul.

He pulled her into an embrace, and Catherine clung to him willingly. "You always understand, Catherine. See, this is why I look forward to Thursdays, the best of all the week."

Catherine's heart contracted painfully for a moment as she stood there, Micah's strong arms around her, as though nothing else in the world mattered.

But as he spoke, he had reminded her that they were not the only people in the world. There were others—other lovers.

She was not the only one that soothed Micah, that held him when frustrated, who he poured out his heart to. But she could not think about that, she would not. Right now, she was all he had, and he was all she had. All she needed.

Catherine's eyelashes flickered at the intensity of this moment. His hands were on her waist, tugging her closer, and there was nothing she wanted more than—

"Now," said Micah, pulling away to look into her eyes with a wry smile. "I didn't come here to complain all night, I promise."

Catherine grinned. "I wouldn't complain if you did, you know."

He rolled his eyes. "You probably should."

"The day I complain to you is the day I lose you."

She had tried to give her statement a lilting air, something akin to a tease, despite the truth in it.

Catherine knew Micah came to her because she did not complain. Their encounters were for Micah and for him alone. Her needs, her wants…beyond what Micah could give her with his fingers, his mouth, and his manhood, were not important.

It only cut into her heart on other days, when he was gone and she was left to face a week without him.

Not that she was in love with him, Catherine reminded herself silently as Micah laughed at what he presumed was her jest. Absolutely not. She would not have been so foolish as to fall in love with a gentleman.

"Kiss me," Catherine breathed.

The request had poured from her mouth before she could stop it. Micah grinned, that dark mischievous grin she knew so well, and eagerly captured her lips with his own.

She whimpered, clutching at him tighter as his tongue took possession of her. There was nothing like it, the heady sensations he sparked in her, the sense of being utterly possessed, the growing, aching need inside her that made everything—

"Catherine," moaned Micah.

Catherine's fingers tightened around his neck, entangling in his hair. "Micah."

All she had been able to do was breathe his name; there was no other air in her lungs, it was being entirely taken by his passionate kisses—kisses that would lead to—

Micah broke the kiss. "I have such tension in my shoulders, Cat."

She smiled. "Well, thank goodness I know a cure for that."

Within minutes, she had stripped off his coat, waistcoat, and shirt, and the man was lying on her bed face down, his head tucked sideways on a pillowcase that had been recently laundered.

Catherine tried not to notice the shabby sheet on the bed, the slightly torn fabric falling down the four poster that would need her seamstress skills tomorrow, now she'd noticed.

Instead, she clambered onto the bed, carefully straddled Micah, and lowered herself down to sink her hands onto his shoulders.

"Micah de Petras," she said in a stern, mocking tone. "Your shoulders are tied in so many knots, you could go to sea! Why didn't you come to me immediately?"

His flesh was taut, not an inch of fat on him. Catherine swallowed. The muscles she moved with her hands fought against her. He was all man.

Micah groaned happily, and Catherine swallowed down her instinct to ask him to make her moan in just such a way. Patience was a virtue, after all, and if she did her job well, she was all the more likely to enjoy the pleasure he would bestow on her later.

"I came to you as soon as I saw my family," came the befuddled reply of a blissful Micah. "Besides, I only see you on Thursdays, you know that."

Concentrating on a particularly hard knot, Catherine murmured, "I know."

That had been the arrangement; and in truth, it had benefited her at the time. Every Thursday at six o'clock—unless he was late, which in fairness was an irregularity. Micah would arrive at her rooms, they would talk, laugh, sometimes eat together, and always make love.

And he would be gone by the time she awoke. A note would always be left, along with a ten-pound note. And that would be it for the week.

"Mmm," breathed Micah. "Oh, yes. That's the spot."

Her fingers worked deftly to release the tension. How did one man gain such tension in just seven days? A man with ten pounds a week to spend on his mistress, and goodness knows how many other women. It was hard to believe that such a terrible and yet wealthy life could exist.

"Oh, I am so glad it is Thursday," murmured Micah, eyes closed and a smile dancing on his face as Catherine's hands moved across his shoulders to his neck. "Of all my mistresses, you always know how to make me feel better."

A prickle of irritation worked its way down Catherine's spine. *Of all his mistresses?*

She had known she was compared to the others, in small ways at least. It was natural when one was a better conversationalist, or another attired herself in more impressive gowns.

But to hear it spoken aloud, during such a moment as this…

Catherine forced a smile. "I suppose I am the best mistress you have ever had?"

"The best."

"And my fingers don't have anything to do with that, do they?"

"Oh, they have everything to do with it," Micah murmured. "Please, don't stop."

Catherine swallowed. A warm pit of desire was building in her stomach as she continued to touch, stroke, and soothe the handsome man between her legs, but she knew better than to make a demand of him. Oh no, Micah was the one who dictated when they made love. It had always been that way.

She could not think of that. She had to distract herself. Think of something else.

"So, what happened this evening, then?" Catherine asked quietly.

"I don't want to talk about it."

"Yes, I rather presumed that," she said dryly. Did his other mistresses talk to him like this? Could they be as direct as she, as bold as she? "But I rather think you need to."

Finding a particularly sore part of his shoulder, Catherine gently eased out the knots.

"Christ!"

"And if you don't let it out now, you'll only come back to me in worse pain next week," Catherine continued as though she had not just made a man spasm underneath her by the merest touch of a finger. "Come on, Micah. You know you can talk to me."

She had lowered her voice to a seductive timbre she knew he loved so well.

Micah opened one eye and glanced up. "You think?"

Catherine shook her head with a wry smile. "I know."

He groaned, closed his eye, and turned his head to the other side. She waited, knowing that if she gave him enough time—

"It's my family again," Micah sighed. "Pushing me to get onto the marriage market. Me! A husband! Can you see me the happy husband of a foolish bride?"

Catherine absolutely refused to permit herself to think about it. "You know, I can't imagine it."

Micah snorted, as though that proved his point. "Yet my mother will not stop going on about it, on and on, as though she could simply wear me down by consistently demanding that I marry! It's outrageous!"

"It usually works," pointed out Catherine. Slipping off her straddling position to the bed beside him, she laughed at his outraged expression. "I am not saying you should give in, not at all! But you must admit, most people eventually give into such pressure. Did not your sister?"

"Emerald?" Micah made a face as he turned onto his side. "I don't understand her, but then I never have. But she isn't me, Cat. I mean it, I have far too much fun with you and the others to think about settling down."

Catherine nodded, though she said nothing. It would be imprudent of her to point out, after all, that matrimony hardly seemed to prevent most men from seeing their mistresses. Indeed, for some men, it rather made it easier.

"And Coral just stands there looking like butter that won't melt," sighed Micah. "As though she knows what's best for me when she hardly knows me!"

"And whose fault is that?"

"Oh, mine, I suppose?" Micah said. "Well, it probably is my fault, but then Coral is hardly the easiest person to get along with."

"Whereas you are a dream."

"Thank you," said Micah with a mock bow.

Catherine giggled. He was such a fool, and he knew it, that was the best of it all. He would have his speeches, arguments, and shouts, but if she or anyone else was foolish enough to say anything against any of his sisters, Micah would be the first person to roundly defend them.

With fists, if need be.

"I suppose I shall have to go and apologize to my mother tomorrow for leaving in such a huff."

Catherine shrugged, lifting a hand to cup his cheek. "You do not have to."

"Oh, but I do," he said with a sigh. "You don't know my family. I think I'll be fortunate if I am not expected to apologize to Coral, too."

"Coral?"

"She is the heir, and I…wasn't particularly polite about it."

Catherine said nothing. Micah had tried to explain this to her before, of course, but she had never entirely understood it. A woman the head of the family? It happened sometimes, of course, if a husband was called away, taken to war, lost. But the head of the family while the husband was still living?

It was an interesting idea.

"You know, I did not believe I would be able to enjoy this evening," said Micah suddenly. "But I already am. You do something in me, Catherine, something no one else does."

Her heart skipped a beat, even as Catherine attempted to tell herself not to see within his words something that was not there. *He did not care for her like that, he—*

"And now," Micah added, "I am absolutely starving."

Catherine shivered slightly with anticipation. Well, she knew what those hands could do, that mouth, that manhood—

"I am afraid I have very little food in the place," she whispered, creeping into his arms and moaning at the intense warmth of his body.

Micah grinned. "Wonderful. I'll just have to have you."

When Catherine awoke the next morning, aching after their frantic and eager lovemaking that continued into the early hours of the morning, it was to see an empty place in the bed next to her.

She swallowed, pain rising in her chest. *He was gone.*

Of course he was. She had to expect that; that was the arrangement, after all. This was not a marriage. They were two people who enjoyed each other's company, one of whom paid to keep the other.

Catherine glanced over to the console table by the door. On it, even from this distance, she could see a folded note, short, and a ten-pound note.

Sighing, she leaned back into the tumbled linens of her bed. Micah de Petras. A gentleman like none other she had ever met. A man who had swiftly, over the last few years, taken over all her thoughts and hopes and dreams.

A man who kissed like the devil and made love like one, too.

A smile crept across Catherine's face. Perhaps it was time for this to come to an end.

Not to stop seeing Micah; oh no, that was quite the opposite of her intention.

"It's my family again. Pushing me to get onto the marriage market. Me! A husband! Can you see me the happy husband of a foolish bride?"

Catherine swallowed. She certainly could see him as a husband, *her* husband.

Though she was expertly adept at seducing Micah's body, perhaps it was time to consider seducing his heart. She would have to be determined, he was not a man for the catching, as he had so elegantly proven.

But she would have him. Catherine Tetlow would be more than a mistress.

CHAPTER THREE

September 8, 1812

"—AND THERE'S THE king!"

Cries rang out around the table as those who won cheered, cheeks flushed and eyes bright, and those who had lost threw back their heads in outrage, hands waving as though that could change the cards on the table.

Micah threw down his cards with disgust and swallowed the last of the ale in his tankard.

A king! It was outrageous, the chances of the man turning up was…well, he could hardly work it out now, not with a second pint of ale in him, but still. It felt impossible. He had been holding out for a queen for what felt like the entire night, ever since they had sat at this godforsaken table.

The five shillings he had placed on the table were scooped up by some blaggard who had a tooth missing, though that did not prevent him from grinning.

A nudge to his shoulder. Micah turned irritably to glare at his companion.

"You lost again," pointed out James Gresley, Earl of Maltravers, in that irritatingly calm conversational tone he always had.

Micah glowered, not bothering to give him a response.

This had been a mistake. It had all felt like such a good idea a few hours ago. The man had turned up at his rooms, mooning about some girl he liked—not that Micah had paid much attention, in truth—and the only way he could be shut up was dragging him to a gambling den.

There were four gambling dens within walking distance—comfortable walking distance, which to Micah typically meant staggering distance back in the early hours—and one was rather unfortunately closed.

Something to do with smuggling. Micah had not bothered to ask too closely; he hardly needed the *ton* to catch onto the idea that he frequented it, after all. Everyone talked—and worse, everyone talked to his mother.

So, he had pulled James, moaning still about this woman and how no one was willing to help him land her, to his favorite gambling den.

Micah had intended it to be a splendid evening, preferably for himself. It was not that he was a bad loser, it was more that he rarely had any opportunity to experience it. Cards were what he knew. He was rather good at them.

Until someone like this blaggard cheated…

Micah glared silently at the chuckling man who was receiving pats on the back from his fellows as he poured the money into his pockets.

His pockets! The layabout did not even have a pocketbook to hold the damn spoils!

Very suspect, if anyone asked him; but Micah was not foolish enough to start throwing accusations of cheating about in a place like this. Not if he wanted to be able to stagger home, three pints of ale in the future, in one piece.

"Micah?"

Micah blinked. *James was still trying to talk to him.* "What?" he snapped defensively.

The earl raised his hands in mock surrender as people left the gaming table and others took their place. "Hold fire, old man, I did not intend to—"

"I'm just annoyed, that's all."

"You don't say," said James coolly.

Micah swallowed. It was most irritating, but there it was. When one had known someone as long as James—there were only four years between them, after all, and they had grown up alongside each other.

When the old earl had died suddenly, leaving the boy orphaned...well, James had been near eighteen, so the courts let him merely assume his majority early. Wasn't that how it was? Micah could hardly remember.

James had everything he wanted. Freedom. The chance to make one's decisions—the headship of his family!

Not that it had helped him win at cards, though.

"I should have won," Micah muttered.

James's eyes widened immediately, and he glanced about to ensure no one else had heard. "You cannot just say—"

"I can say what I think," said Micah boldly, knowing it was a mistake but saying it anyway. "Who will argue with me?"

He had raised his voice a little, like the fool he was. That was the trouble with the heat of the moment; you could just about see yourself being a complete cad, but you didn't seem to be able to stop yourself.

The gaming den was rammed. People at every table, others standing watching them. The bar was sticky, gleaming in the candlelight, and men shouted their orders as the poor barmaids attempted to pour three glasses at once.

Smoke filled the place, cigars pouring out different scents to the point of overwhelming. A few ladies—and there were ladies, though Micah thought he should probably call them women. No lady of any repute would be found here. Women, then, wandered around the tables, smiling. The smiles themselves altered depending on who they were looking at.

Some of the older men received smiles of encouragement and support. The women tried to sit on their laps, squawking about being good luck charms.

The younger gentlemen, on the other hand, received smiles of seduction. A few had already succumbed, and Micah had watched them be led out with cheers from their fellows.

Others, like James, appeared to be totally immune.

Micah shook his head ruefully. The man must truly be besotted with this…this whoever it was. He could not recall the name of the lady James had given his heart to now, but she must be impressive if the earl could ignore so many pretty young things wandering past, giving him the eye.

"Again?"

Micah blinked. A man to his left on the other side of James was looking at the pair of them with the deck of cards in his hand, half the table dealt.

"I'm game if you are," said James cheerfully, as though he had nothing to lose.

Micah sighed. And in a very real way, he did not. Why, the man had his own fortune, a title, and no family to bow down to or take orders from.

Heaven.

Whereas he…

Micah surreptitiously placed a hand in his pocket. There was one coin left.

He rose, almost knocking the chair over. "No, I tire of this table. Come on, James."

James did not hesitate to follow his friend, for which Micah supposed he should feel grateful. It was not usually a good idea to come to a place like this without a friend, someone to watch your back. Not that it was the most dangerous place he ever frequented, but still. One could never be too careful.

"You lost," said his friend blandly as they moved to a table that three men had just left. "You just have to accept it."

Micah snorted. Catching the eye of a rather harassed-looking barmaid, he jerked his head. Within a moment, she had carried over two more pints of ale.

"He's getting this round," he muttered.

James sighed, pulled out a coin, and thrust it at the woman. "Micah—"

"Don't you Micah me," said Micah warningly. "I get enough of that from my parents."

"Oh, don't be so bitter."

All too late, Micah remembered. Of course. James had lost his mother at birth, and with his father now gone…he was alone.

"Forgive me."

"It's nothing," said James shortly, his voice revealing it most certainly was not nothing.

Micah sighed heavily and took a long, deep drink of his ale. All of a sudden, the blasted thing was empty. "It's just—I am no earl, nor a man with a fortune. I cannot just afford to lose money!"

He regretted his openness immediately, and instead of looking up at his companion, chose to look down into his drink. His empty drink.

Well, it was hardly the conversation one wanted to have with anyone, even a friend like James who knew most, if not all of his faults.

Poverty, as a gentleman—a gentleman from a wealthy family, a family the whole of Society knew was rolling in money—was not something one was ever supposed to admit.

Micah swallowed. It was not something he liked to think about, let alone discuss, but now the subject had been opened…

James cleared his throat. "Well, I mean to say…I know things are different with the de Petras family, different from most families in fact, but—"

"You don't know the half of it, and I wish you would not speak on it," snapped Micah.

Oh, it was all too easy to have a short temper with a friend, wasn't it? He saw the hurt on James's face, saw him swallow down whatever words of comfort and support he was going to offer, and felt wretched.

A cheer came up from the table they had just left. The man

with the missing tooth had won again.

Micah clenched a hand but attempted to console himself with the thought that he had made the right decision to leave the table. Something was fixed over there, and even if he could not name it, he knew it. He had saved himself the only coin he had left, at the very least.

Glancing back at James, he was about to say something but closed his mouth. His friend looked…well, miserable. He would not like to suggest such a thing, but it was remarkable just how dour the man looked.

Damn. Damn and blast. His stupid mouth—that was perhaps one thing he had in common with Coral; the ability to speak first and think about it later, if at all.

Perhaps that was why they were so frequently at odds with each other.

Sighing heavily, Micah did the only thing he knew how to when it came to things like this. He apologized. Badly.

He nudged James heavily. "You know I did not mean that."

"Oh, I think you did."

Micah rolled his eyes. "Damnit man—you do know us, you know us better than almost anyone in Society. Sometimes I think you understand the de Petras family better than anyone in it."

A wry smile crept across James's face. "Probably."

"And you are good to our family," Micah said. *Well, it was hardly a secret, was it?* There were several drawing rooms that the de Petras family would not be welcome in if it were not for the gentle hints laid down by the Earl of Maltravers—or, heaven forbid, Lady Romeril. "Without you, I think we would be in a pretty dire situation half the time, don't you?"

"*You* certainly would be."

"Go away with you," said Micah with a dry laugh. "No, I think of all of us, it's Sapphire we've got to worry about."

A strange look came over James's face. Not embarrassment, but a red tinge covered his cheeks. "Sapphy?"

"Sapphy indeed. Coral and Emerald are married, after all,"

pointed out Micah fairly, "so they can be their own husbands' problems now, but Sapphire…"

Micah stared. His gaze had been casually drifting across the gaming den. His eyes had taken in a multitude of different people; old men with gray hair, men so young they should better be called boys, a few more women in tatty gowns and seductive smiles, attempting to get what little coin they could…and Catherine.

He blinked; it could not be her. She would not be here.

But it was absolutely and unmistakably her. There was no one else in the world who had hair like that—a golden that seemed to shimmer even in this dull, dank place. Its curls were natural, as far as Micah could make out—at least, he had never seen her curl it.

She was beautiful. Oh, he had always known she was a pretty woman, that was the reason he had first made his offer to her. But here, in the gaming den, her beauty took on another level of radiance. She seemed to shine, to glow in the darkness, the smoke around her making her look ethereal. Too beautiful to be real. Her lips were red, and they were curled in a smile. *A smile at someone else.*

Micah's stomach lurched. She was…Catherine was talking to the man with the missing tooth, on their old table! She was smiling, her attention entirely focused on him as he spoke, and then she laughed.

She laughed!

Micah's hands became fists as shock and jealousy roared through his chest. How dare she! Smile and laugh, and with that rogue!

Though with any rogue, now he came to think about it, that would be impossible for him to accept. Speak with someone else, like that? That careful, intimate way he had with her—to see it before him, with another man, it was intolerable!

Catherine Tetlow…flirting?

It was impossible to understand what to do with himself.

Micah felt set apart in a strange way, unable to speak, unable to move, merely watching the outrageous sight.

Only able to watch his Catherine—and when she had precisely become his Catherine, he was not sure—tease another man.

It had to be stopped.

"Micah?" said James curiously as Micah stood up, hands still clenched. "What are you—Micah!"

Micah did not heed his friend. Not with this boiling hot ache within him that absolutely had to be stopped. She had to be stopped.

The man with the missing tooth looked up as Micah approached. "Come to try to win a bit of your money back, eh?"

Micah ignored him. All his attention was focused on the stunningly beautiful woman beside him, who had straightened up and put a hand on her hips.

"Micah de Petras," Catherine said sensuously with a raised eyebrow.

It was all he could do to prevent his manhood from immediately standing to attention. Dear God, that's what it always had done when he was faced with Catherine, wasn't it? But this was unheard of, he had never seen her outside her rooms.

That was where Catherine existed, and there she existed only for him.

But to find her here…

"Come with me," he said firmly.

She was given little choice. Exclaiming at the suddenness of the movement, Catherine was pulled away from the table to the wall by Micah's strong hands.

"I don't want you to do that," he said fiercely.

Catherine gently removed his hand, and Micah almost cried out at her touch. Oh, he craved her as he could not remember doing so before. But this was not Thursday, his body was not expecting to taste the sweetness of Catherine today.

Was it?

"Do what?" Catherine asked lightly, her eyes dancing.

Micah almost growled, "You know precisely what."

The loud chatter and laughter of the gaming den rose around them, but Micah only had eyes and ears for her. Everything else faded away, becoming a roar like the ocean in the background of his mind.

Catherine smiled wickedly. "You don't like me leaving my rooms?"

"It's not that, you know it's—"

"You don't like me attending gaming dens?"

Micah swallowed. He didn't, now it came to that, but there was no rational reason why, and he could hardly think straight as it was.

It was just...*wrong*. Wrong, that was the only way he could think to describe it. It was wrong that Catherine was here, without him—but no, it wasn't that, was it? Because he wouldn't bring her here in the first place. He would keep her in his rooms, make love to her, feel her beneath him, and above him, and—

"You have other mistresses, I think?" Catherine asked lightly.

Micah's stomach clenched. "And what is that supposed to mean?"

She shrugged, the movement causing Micah's attention to be caught by the rather sumptuous suggestion of her breasts.

He swallowed.

"Well, I merely mean you bestow your favors to others, and I..." Catherine allowed her voice to gently fall away.

Nausea rose in Micah's stomach. She could not be suggesting—surely, she did not mean she permitted herself to be bedded by other men?

They had never agreed on any sort of...of exclusivity, of course. That would have required Micah to give up his other ladies, something he would have laughed at if she had been foolish enough to suggest it.

Micah's eye caught the hungry expression of the man with a missing tooth, looking over at them. At Catherine.

His stomach lurched most painfully. "That is not the same."

"Why not?" Catherine asked.

Micah opened his mouth but had absolutely nothing to say, then closed it again.

Why not? Why not? It should be obvious to her—it certainly was to him, even if he could not explain it.

It was agony to see her here, watch her smile at another man.

He had never seen any of his mistresses act like that in public. Now he came to think about it, Micah was not sure whether he had ever seen any of his mistresses in public, save Annie that one time at Emerald's wedding, and that had been a jest.

He may be the black sheep of the family, but he was no fool.

"Catherine," he murmured.

Her gaze caught his, and something hot and painful and wonderful shot through Micah like a bullet.

It rocked him, almost causing him to fall. It was a good thing they were standing so close to the wall, sticky and grimy as it was, as he was able to lean on it and prevent his feet from giving way.

What on earth was that?

"I…" Micah tried to say.

Catherine's smile widened. It was rather too knowing for Micah's liking, and when she spoke, it was in that warm, slow, gentle way that made all his bones melt.

All, save one.

"Micah de Petras," she said softly, "I am beginning to think you are…jealous."

Micah stiffened. "Nonsense."

The response had been immediate, even if it was a lie. *Jealous? Him?* Micah had never been jealous in his entire life, save for James's wealth and title, and that was natural.

Jealous about Catherine? That could not be what this feeling, whatever it was, could be.

"Look," he said desperately, "all I ask is that you stay away from other men. I do not think that is too much to ask, I treat you well, don't I?"

There was a small hesitation from Catherine before she said,

"You do."

"I do," said Micah. "Yes. Good. So, I do not think it unreasonable to ask that you stay away from other men. You agree, of course?"

The smile on Catherine's face made his stomach lurch again, and it broadened as she said, quite gently and calmly, "No."

CHAPTER FOUR

September 11, 1812

CATHERINE CAREFULLY TUCKED the second ten-pound note into her corset.

Well, it was unlikely anyone was going to look there as she walked down the street, she thought ruefully as she pulled on a pelisse that had seen better autumns.

In fact, now she came to look at it, the stitching all along one side was mere moments away from coming apart.

She tried hard not to look in the looking glass. She would have to add her pelisse to the pile of mending—a pile of mending quickly increasing with every passing week. She needed to purchase another needle, the one she had was barely sharp enough now to make it through the fabric…and she needed more fabric, now she came to think of it.

Catherine sighed. She could not think of all that today, for today was a day for laughter, and joy, and a time to see some of the people who meant the most to her.

Not a day to count how carefully she was hanging by a literal thread.

As she closed the door to her rooms behind her, locking the door and placing the key in the same safe place she had placed her money—right in her corset—Catherine heard someone clear their throat meaningfully.

For a moment, she closed her eyes, sighed, then took a deep breath. She could do this. It would be a short conversation, and then she would be gone.

Opening her eyes and smiling brightly, Catherine turned to smile at her neighbor. "Mrs. Goldsmith."

Mrs. Goldsmith grinned. "Miss Tetlow."

Catherine bobbed a curtsey as quick as she could manage and immediately started walking down the corridor—but she was halted by her words.

"Going somewhere?"

That was the trouble with neighbors. They had a rather disobliging habit of being interested in one.

Turning on her heels, Catherine said primly, "Yes. Good day."

She had almost reached the staircase when the woman spoke again. "Going where?"

Catherine tried to take another deep breath as she placed her hand on the banister, attempting to make it as clear as possible she did not have the time to stand around chattering away. She was very busy. *She had an appointment.*

But there was no real harm in Mrs. Goldsmith, and in fact, there was typically a great deal of good. The woman had been kind to her when she had first moved to the building, and a young woman who lived alone was ripe for scandal.

Mrs. Goldsmith had never spread anything about her. As far as she knew.

"Just to visit some friends, Mrs. Goldsmith," Catherine said lightly, taking a step down the stairs. "I wish you a good day."

She may have said something more, but she could not hear from halfway down the staircase, and Catherine ensured to reach it as soon as possible. There had once been carpet here, a dark green, if the threadbare remains were anything to go by. But the carpet had been worn away a good deal of time ago, and now it was almost entirely wood.

Much like the rest of Parson's Buildings, the staircase had seen better days.

Catherine remembered to jump the last one—a thin piece of pine had been placed in the hole someone had created a few weeks ago, but it creaked most ominously, and she had no wish for her ankle to be caught—and felt her shoulders relax as she stepped out onto the street.

Warm autumnal air and the scent of a pie seller's wares filled her nostrils. This was her favorite time of year, though she would have to admit that the state of her lodgings were perhaps the reason for that. Too hot in summer, freezing in winter and spring, it was only autumn that the place felt habitable.

Catherine pulled her pelisse tighter as she stepped onto the bustling pavement. She supposed, when she had been younger, she'd had a favorite season independent of one's ability to keep warm. She could not recall it.

The journey she took was one she knew well, and Catherine's mind was able to wander as her feet took her along the streets, lanes, and alleyways that would take her to the McCalls.

"I do not think it unreasonable to ask that you stay away from other men. You agree, of course?"

"No."

A wry smile crept across Catherine's face as she carefully crossed the road, dodging a barouche being driven by an absolute maniac.

Well, she had not expected Micah to be at that particular gaming den, but it had been remarkably convenient that he was. His reaction was precisely what she had hoped for; jealousy and possessiveness, the like she had never seen before.

"I don't want you to do that…"

But then, Catherine reminded herself as she stepped along the street, heart racing, he had never seen her out in public, had he? That alone must have been a surprise. Did he think she was trapped in those rooms all hours of the day?

He could not be more wrong.

She knocked sharply on the door as she arrived, and it was opened almost immediately, as she knew it would.

"You are almost late," said Mrs. McCall with a stern look.

Catherine bobbed a curtsey—lower than the one she had graced Mrs. Goldsmith with—and nodded. "Yet I think you will find I am right on—"

The church chimes at the end of the street muffled her words but proved her point.

Mrs. McCall sniffed. "I suppose so. You have it?"

Catherine did not need to ask the woman what she meant; she always wanted the same thing every week, and every week Catherine had it. Mostly.

She pulled the two ten-pound notes from her corset and wished they were not quite so warm as she handed them over to the older woman. "For September."

Mrs. McCall shook her head. "You were three pounds short for August."

"Which I will have for you soon," Catherine said hastily, her stomach twisting. She had hoped she would forget about that, but she should have known. "Next week, in fact."

If she'd had a thicker pelisse, one with longer sleeves, she could have crossed her fingers within it and hoped Mrs. McCall would not see, but as it was, she could only lie.

Well, she would have it, wouldn't she? Micah would be visiting soon, and her rent of two pounds would come from that ten pounds, and she would have to buy a little more firewood, and food…and some fabric, and that damned needle, but after those expenses—

"Come on in, then," said Mrs. McCall, bad-tempered.

She turned and stomped into her home, and Catherine followed her eagerly to see—

"Catty!"

"Catty's here!"

Catherine smiled, her heart warming, all fears and frustrations falling away.

It was worth it; the tension, the scrimping, the careful spending that would keep her cold for a few weeks…to see them smile.

John was sitting at the table, a book before him and a pencil in his hand, while Mary was sitting by the window, evidently looking out for her—in completely the wrong direction, Catherine was delighted to see. The last thing she needed was for her siblings to attempt to find her when she was gone.

"I am indeed here, and glad to see you working at your letters, John," she said warmly as she strode in and opened her arms.

Her little brother and sister ran into her arms, and Catherine clasped them to her, breathing in their clean clothes.

Yes, Mrs. McCall may be gruff, but she did not take the money Catherine so carefully brought her every month and spend it on herself. No, John and Mary were kept safe, warm, fed, and clothed, which was far more than many children of their acquaintance.

It was not enough. But it was enough for now.

"I hate my letters," said John conversationally. "I shan't need them when grown, will I?"

"All the more, I am afraid," Catherine laughed, tucking back a curl of hair past his ear. "And you, Mary, how are your letters coming on?"

"The girl don't learn her letters," came the curt words of Mrs. McCall behind her.

Catherine straightened up and looked at her young sister. "Truly, Mary? You are not attending to your lessons?"

But there was no awkward defensiveness in Mary; instead, she looked rather fearfully at the woman behind her.

Her heart twisting uncomfortably, Catherine turned to look at Mrs. McCall. "Well?"

"She don't learn no letters because she'll have no need of 'em," said Mrs. McCall, sitting in a chair in the little parlor they stood in, pulling what appeared to be a pile of mending onto her lap. "What do a girl need learning for?"

Bitterness bubbled up in Catherine's chest, and she tried hard not to say anything immediately, allowing the anger to rise then hopefully cool before she spoke.

Mrs. McCall was not alone in her estimation, after all. Most of the women Catherine knew—though it was a sorry lot, and certainly not the sort of class she and her siblings had been born to—could not read or write.

But Catherine could. Her mother had been absolutely certain the Tetlows would learn to read and write, go to school. John's name had been down for a grammar school. If it had not been for—

Catherine forced the thought aside. She would not think of it. She would not punish herself with such sad thoughts.

"Anyways, you don't give me enough money for the two of them to learn," continued Mrs. McCall, pointedly looking at the two ten-pound notes she had placed on the large table where John had been sitting. "Them's enough for one lot of learning, I reckon."

Catherine swallowed. "And could Mary not share John's—"

"I said there's only one lot of learning in that money," Mrs. McCall said sharply, and there was a steel in her eyes now that Catherine rarely saw, but recognized. "This ent no charity, Miss Tetlow. I take in your brother and sister for money, and it cost money to keep a child fed, stomachs bottomless as they are. Aye, and clothes they cannot fit within a week, and warmth they need every day...if you had more money, o'course..."

Her voice trailed away delicately, pointedly, and Catherine wished to goodness she could throw down a hundred pounds if it meant little Mary could learn to read and write as she ought.

Better, she wished she had a home of her own, and not two cramped rooms in a building hardly fit for an animal, where she could bring her siblings to grow up in warmth and love.

But that was not the world they lived in. Not yet, at any rate.

Catherine smiled coldly at the woman. "I will have the money I owe you for August next week, and then we can discuss Mary's education."

Mrs. McCall sniffed. "As you say."

Catherine turned to her siblings and saw the disappointment on their faces; knew they had hoped, as they hoped every week, that she would announce she had found a home for them. But it was not to be, not this week, and not for many weeks hence if Catherine did not do something.

Her stomach tightened. *Do something she could regret.*

Her visit, an hour each week as she had agreed with Mrs. McCall, was over swiftly. Too swiftly. There never seemed enough time to hear all their news, their complaints, be caught up with their hopes for the future, and the nightmares which had plagued them.

Catherine kissed away the pain of a graze on her sister's knee, marveling that they were so alike in their desire to run about the place, and helped her brother with a particularly difficult sum that apparently Mrs. McCall had not been able to make heads nor tails of.

And then it was over.

"But you'll be back next week, won't you, Catty?" asked Mary eagerly, eyes wide.

Catherine smiled wistfully. It had been the nickname their father had given her, and her siblings were the only people who used it now, even though she had not liked it at the time. It was a link to a past she could not get back, no matter how much she tried, and it was a stark reminder of what she had lost. What all three of them had lost.

"Of course I will be back next week," she promised, pulling the two of them into her arms for a final embrace. "And you be good, and work on your sums, and—and be polite to Mrs. McCall and her husband," Catherine added, catching the woman's eye.

"Good day, Miss Tetlow," Mrs. McCall said pointedly, opening the front door. "And be sure to come back next week with them three pounds—and if you want to bring October's money ahead of time, I won't complain."

Catherine gritted her teeth as she stepped onto the street and heard the door slam behind her. Yes, she was sure Mrs. McCall would not mind having twenty whole pounds early.

Goodness. Three pounds to find next week, and then within two weeks another twenty pounds—and it was getting colder every day, thought Catherine as she started to walk back to her rooms, less of a spring in her step this direction of her journey.

Colder meant more firewood, and where was she supposed to get such money from?

The obvious answer was one she had attempted to avoid for the last three months, but as the summer disappeared slowly, Catherine had been forced to consider it.

She considered it again as she turned a corner onto a larger road, carefully avoiding a gaggle of young ladies in far more fashionable pelisses than hers, who evidently would not consider lowering themselves to move out of her way.

Another lover. Become the mistress of a second gentleman.

The thought was repellent, but Catherine could conceive of no other option.

Micah gave her ten pounds a week. That was an income of five hundred and twenty a year; not shabby at all for a single lady, but when one had two dependents and difficulty securing respectable lodgings that were also affordable, it was not very much indeed.

But two lovers…

Catherine bit her lip as she continued on, past a haberdashers, two bakeries, an office that looked as though it could be a solicitor, and a few private homes.

A second lover. Someone other than Micah in her bed, in her arms.

What other choice did she have?

She could always ask Micah for more money. Catherine smiled wryly at the thought; Micah was not a man with unlimited funds, and in some ways, he was just as bereft of income as she was. Though she knew better than to ask the details, Micah had spoken enough times of his irritation that he had a small income gifted to him by his mother, and nothing else.

Why, how many times had he spoken of how he had 'borrowed' a hundred pounds—a hundred pounds!—from his mother's bureau, or cadged twenty pounds from one of his sisters, or managed to win fifty from his bookies?

No, she could not ask Micah for an increase in the money he gave her—besides, if she was going to be making demands of Micah, there were other things she wanted from him far more dearly.

His heart, for example.

As Catherine turned onto the widest street in her journey, carriages rattling down it, arguments echoing up the street, laughter and chatter in the late autumn sunlight, she allowed herself—just for a minute—to picture her future. A future, that is, as she would have it.

Micah. Herself and Micah, together, in love—married, perhaps, with a home of their own. A home where Mary and John could live happily, attend school, grow up in warmth and comfort as they deserved.

And after they would go to bed, she and Micah would be left alone downstairs. Alone, and in love, and able to enjoy all the benefits of thick walls and—

Micah.

Catherine blinked. Almost as though she had conjured him up from her own imagination, there was Micah, standing further down the street. No, not standing, walking.

Walking arm in arm with a woman who was laughing at something he had just said.

Jealousy erupted within Catherine's heart, as she had known it would.

Micah, with another one of his mistresses. Well, he hardly hid that he had several, it was no secret between them, however much she may jest that she had no wish to hear about them. But to see him with one of them—

Catherine did not think. Thinking was for those with rationality, and there was nothing rational about what she was feeling.

Striding toward the pair, heart pounding, Catherine smiled coldly as she reached them. "I think not."

Before either Micah or the woman, whoever she was—*harlot*, Catherine thought privately—could say anything, Catherine had wrenched Micah away from the woman and pushed her aside.

"Go on with you," Catherine said, blood boiling and hackles raised. "I need a private word with Mr. de Petras."

The woman's jaw fell open, and she looked immediately at Micah—but Catherine did not wait for him to respond. No, she had no desire to hear this woman's voice, just seeing her was enough.

Thank goodness she knew London so well.

Expertly stepping into an alleyway with Micah's hand in hers, an alleyway almost entirely hidden by the curve of the street and a sign advertising ladies' gloves, Catherine said nothing until they had emerged onto another, far quieter street.

"There," she said, grinning as she released Micah and pretended to dust something off his shoulder. "That's better."

"What was all that about?" Micah said, laughing.

Catherine's heart contracted as she met his smile. Oh, he was so handsome when he smiled like that. How did anyone not fall in love with him the moment they saw him?

Not that she was in love with him, of course.

"You had something on your arm," she said aloud.

"What?"

"A woman that was most unsuitable for you," Catherine said with a wink. "You cannot trust women like that."

Micah shook his head. "Cat, she's just like you!"

"I know," came her quick response as she grinned wickedly. "And I am sure she was about to cheat you or pickpocket you, and I just had to save you for myself."

His laughter was everything she needed, and all she needed, and Catherine gloried in the connection they shared. There was no one like Micah de Petras, no one at all—and if she could have her way, there would be no one for him, either.

"Well, I suppose I cannot argue with that," he was saying. "As long as they are like you, and take from my money and leave my heart alone!"

And all the sunlight disappeared from the day.

"As long as they are like you, and take from my money and leave my heart alone!"

Of course. She was a fool to think she had ever touched Micah's heart. She was a woman to him, a thing to make love to, a port in the storm of his life; somewhere to come to rest and receive pleasure, then he would be on.

She was a fool to think she could ever be more. That she could ever claim his heart.

"Now then," said Micah pleasantly, offering her his arm. "Where shall we go?"

Catherine's insides were tied in knots, but she managed to take his arm with what she hoped was a genuine smile. "I know it is not Thursday, but…"

She tried to put as much sensuality and warmth into those words as possible, and she both saw and felt the reaction within him.

Micah groaned. "You are a temptress, Cat."

Catherine smiled. "I am indeed."

But not enough, she could not help but think. *Not enough.*

CHAPTER FIVE

September 16, 1812

MICAH HAD NOT taken his rooms at the Westgate because they were particularly luxurious. Neither had he taken them because they were in the most affluent and respectable part of town, although the last year had rendered the Westgate reputation a little better.

He had not even taken them because they were located close to his club and his favorite gaming den, which was a happy coincidence.

No. He had taken them because they were cheap and cheerful, and all he could afford on the meager income his mother had offered him.

That meant that though he greatly enjoyed the freedom and independence his rooms offered—Micah often found himself returning, against his will and better judgment, to the place he had intended to escape in the first place.

"Micah!" Jasper's joy was genuine and uncontained as he pulled his son into an embrace. "We did not think to see you again so soon!"

Micah accepted the embrace with as much good grace as he could manage. His father was...well. Very expressive for an Englishman.

He always thought it was because he had married an Italian woman. Micah's mother would never be described as a woman who held her emotions in, after all.

But the older Micah grew, he started to wonder whether, in truth, his father had always been a man who felt things deeply and had never permitted himself to express them until he had married.

"Is that Micah?"

Finally released from his father's clutches, Micah turned to grin at Sapphire, who had rushed into the room, hair wild, with a grin on her face.

"Thank goodness, you have saved me from some very tiresome pianoforte practice," she said with a laugh. "The whole family thanks you."

"Whole family?" repeated Micah, heart sinking.

Blast. He had intended to slip into the place while his mother was out—Opal always had tea with Lady Romeril this time each week—borrow some money off Sapphire, who would always part with it, and then perhaps nap in his old bedchamber upstairs. A quiet visit.

Sapphire rolled her eyes. "It's an expression, Micah, you don't have to fear. It's only Papa, Amy, and I here."

"Amy?" Micah wracked his brains trying to recall a friend called Amy. Had he ever met an Amy?"

"Amethyst, you dolt," said Sapphire good-naturedly.

Micah felt his shoulders relax, hated that he could be so easily riled by the thought of being forced to spend time with his family. Not that he had anything against them. Not really. Not when it came down to it.

"Come, sit," said Jasper, indicating the parlor.

Hesitating only a moment, Micah stepped into the parlor and threw himself unceremoniously onto a sofa. Amethyst was reading in a corner, and he was evidently so uninteresting that she did not even bother to look up.

"I thought you were starting to get rather good on the pianoforte, Sapphy," he said conversationally as his youngest sister sat opposite. "Well. Not as terrible as before, I mean."

If he'd said that to Coral, there'd be outrage.

But Sapphire merely laughed. "Yes, I suppose I was rather awful, but then Coral was never very good either, and I don't think Emerald ever truly learned."

"Anything to avoid the spotlight," added Jasper as he sat back by the window and picked up a book with a bookmark in it.

"I don't think Ems is that afraid of attention," said the naïve Sapphire.

Micah snorted. If Emerald could retreat from the world with her husband and child, Beryl, who in his mind did look precisely like her cousin Amber, he was certain she would, and she would probably be much better for it.

"Anyway, Coral says I only have to learn three pieces each Season, and I've almost perfected one."

It was all he could do not to utter a rude remark. *Coral says?* What power Coral had over the youngest de Petras sibling—why was she dictating what Sapphire should do or say in polite Society?

Micah's jaw clenched for a moment, but he managed to relax it.

"I think it's impressive that you're playing anything at all, considering your stub," Jasper pointed out from the window.

Sapphire merely shrugged as a response, but Micah's eyes were drawn to her right hand. Or at least, where her hand would have been if her arm did not end at the wrist.

Goodness, he had almost forgotten. But that was the thing with Sapphire, one did forget. She had been born without a right hand, and the other de Petras children had been raised to understand that it made no difference to who Sapphire was as a person.

As far as Micah could tell, the only difference it actually made was that she got in an awful tangle with bonnet strings if left to her own devices.

"The question is," said Micah aloud, a mischievous grin creeping over his face, "would you consider learning duets with old James?"

"James?" Sapphire blinked for a moment, then laughed. "Oh, Maltravers! Have you heard him sing, absolutely awful!"

"Who is absolutely awful?"

Micah sighed, a nerve in his temple pulsing as the familiar tone echoed in the parlor.

Of course. Of course, he couldn't just come and visit his father—and Sapphire, of course, and Amethyst, though she hardly counted—and enjoy a simple visit. It had to get complicated. It had to involve—

"Coral!" said Sapphire, surprised. "We weren't expecting you until this afternoon."

"Well, I thought I'd come a little early, I knew none of you would mind," Coral said, breezing into the room as though she still lived here, happy as you please.

Micah tried to smile at his sister, but it probably turned out a grimace. "Coral."

"Micah," she said coolly. "Hullo, Papa."

It was only when Coral approached their father for an embrace that Micah realized why Coral had been holding her arm at such a funny angle. It was almost as though—

"Did you have to bring that with you?"

Coral straightened up from embracing their father and blinked, confused. "That?"

Micah nodded. "That."

Sapphire giggled, pursing her lips together as though attempting to hold back her mirth, but she was not succeeding in the slightest. Amethyst seemed to understand the joke, too, though Micah did not think he had said anything amusing.

"That?" repeated Coral, utterly perplexed. Then she looked down at what she was holding in her arms, and her outrage exploded. "You—you mean my *baby?*"

Micah sighed. He knew he should have held his tongue.

There was never anything to be gained by speaking to new mothers. He had learned that a few years ago, when attempting to renew an…acquaintance, he had always maintained it had been an acquaintance, with a lady who had once been a Miss Marnion.

She was married by then, of course, with a babe in arms, and Micah had thought this the perfect opportunity for them to renew their intimacy. She, however, had not.

In fact, she had the same expression as his sister Coral did now. A mixture of outrage, confusion, utter shock, and disbelief.

"You cannot be serious," hissed Coral, evidently unwilling to raise her voice with a sleeping baby in her arms.

Sapphire giggled again, and Amethyst joined her. Micah threw them a wink.

"This is not funny!"

"Coral, I am sure Micah is only teasing," interjected Jasper hurriedly. "You know your brother has a very different sense of humor to—"

"To all of us," came a quiet voice.

Micah groaned. *Emerald was here as well?* He could not have timed this worse if he tried!

"Emerald!" Jasper smiled, delighted, and Micah knew precisely why.

Having all four of his children under one roof was something their father adored. It was one of the few reasons Micah agreed to attend the monthly family dinner, to keep the man happy.

"Did I hear Emerald?"

Micah groaned again. How was it fair that he purposefully chose a morning when his mother would be out of the house, but instead—

"Opal! You're back early," said Jasper, his smile if anything only growing wider. "We're all here!"

Trying his best to keep his face as neutral as possible, Micah allowed the wash of familial noise to surround him.

"You know, it is good we are all together," said Opal over the noise. "I—that is to say, we have something important to tell you. Discuss with you, I suppose."

Coral and Emerald ceased their uncomfortable conversation and turned to look at their mother. Sapphire twisted on the sofa, and Amethyst placed her book down. Even Micah sat up straighter.

This sounded serious, and there was a rather serious look on their mother's face as she stood by their father, the autumnal light from the window highlighting them in a stage-like manner.

Something to discuss with them? Micah could not think what such a topic could be, but if it was important, surely it would be shared only with Coral. If it was not important, why bother to tell them at all? It was most strange.

"Your father and I have been talking," said Opal into the silence. "About our wills."

Micah stared, glanced quickly at Coral, who looked just as astonished as he felt, then returned his gaze to their parents.

Wills? Talking about their wills?

This was all because of Amethyst, there could be no other reason. Try as he might, Micah could not help but glance over at his cousin, whose cheeks were reddening.

Micah could hardly believe it. Change their wills? But what to—and why? Coral would inherit, she was the heir; that was the way it had always been. He had grown up knowing it, knowing he would not precisely be cut off, but would certainly not receive the bulk of the family fortune.

But was that all about to change? Had Amethyst finally convinced his mother to hand over some of the family fortune?

This was not something he had expected. After desiring control over his own destiny, as so many of his friends and acquaintances had, it was rather disconcerting to think that he may be receiving it.

Micah swallowed. "You don't have to—"

"Wills?" repeated Coral, her gaze narrowed on her mother. "You mean you're going to change your will?"

"Yes," said Jasper quietly.

Micah heard a little cry of surprise from Sapphire. He glanced at Emerald, whose face was astonished but who was, as ever, completely silent.

"Why?"

The entire room was looking at him, even Sapphire, and heat rushed into his cheeks.

Why in heavens had he spoke aloud? He should have just let his sisters ask the questions, and he could sit back and absorb the answers. He did not wish to get involved!

Because that was the trouble, wasn't it? None of them could ask the question that was on their hearts, not with Amethyst here.

Was it her? Was their cousin's reappearance last year a catalyst for this change?

"Yes, why?" said Coral, turning to their parents. "Have I done something wrong?"

Micah sighed heavily. *Of course—he should have expected it. Coral does not actually care who gets the money, the shipping business, the houses in Bath their mother rented out. She does not need the prestige, the power—she was a duchess now, for goodness sake!*

Could she not see that the reason was quite obvious, even if they did not understand the impact yet? It was Amethyst. She had turned up here, demanding money, and though she had been peculiarly reticent on that topic recently, surely her request still stood.

No, she was more worried about whether she had done something to upset or offend their parents. Coral de Petras, always needing to be liked, always needing to be in everyone's good books…

"—haven't actually made a final decision," Opal was saying, "but we will let you know soon precisely what—"

"Is it because of Amethyst?" asked Sapphire eagerly. "Have we come into money? Is Papa in debt—is there a debt of honor that—"

"Sapphire!" Micah said heavily.

His voice had chorused with Coral's, and for a moment, their eyes met and there was a sense of understanding there.

And then it was gone.

"I can leave if you would rather discuss this as—well, a family," came the awkward voice of Amethyst. "I don't have to—"

"You don't have to tell us, you know." That was Emerald, her voice quiet and low. "If you do not wish to, it is your own business precisely what your wills…"

Micah rose carefully and saw that none of his family noticed him. Jasper was trying to convince Sapphire that he was not, in actuality, a pirate, and Opal was trying to explain to Emerald why they wanted to wait to tell their children their decision, and to Coral why there had not been a decision yet. Amethyst merely sat there, cheeks pink.

He could not take any more. More de Petras drama, more arguments…it was the same old story, and Micah was sick of it. He'd had enough.

The cold September air hit his face most uncomfortably as he stepped outside the house. Dear God, to think that he had considered this a quiet visit!

In fact, all he'd done was step into another mire. Well, they'd be talking about this one for weeks. The de Petras wills to be changed! Changed to what, changed why, changed to benefit whom?

Micah sighed heavily and leaned against the wall. Sapphire would be going on about this, and he would be dragged into the conversation more times than he would care to admit. Well, he would just have to avoid the place until—

"Five and twenty minutes."

Micah stood up hastily but smiled as the speaker stepped across the street, a grin on her face.

It was Catherine.

"I beg your pardon?"

"Five and twenty minutes," she repeated. "That is how long you managed to stay in there. Is that a familial record?"

Micah sighed, shaking his head. "I suppose so, but I had not expected my sisters—all of them—to be here."

Then his mind caught up with him. *Catherine, here?* Had he ever told her where his parents' home was—and even if he had, what was she doing here?

Catherine appeared to read his mind. Her red lips creased into another smile as a breeze tugged at her blonde curls. "You mentioned you had a visit and I thought...well. You may need some moral support."

A wave of relief poured through Micah. To have someone on his side, on his team, as it were, here...well, he may have been able to stick it out longer in the parlor, if he had known he had Catherine's welcoming arms to fall into the moment that he left.

"You are truly the most impressive woman I have ever met," said Micah.

It was spoken honestly, from the heart, and he could not understand why his words caused a flush across Catherine's face. Of all his mistresses, she was the most attuned to him, but also the most aware of herself, of her powers. Why did she suddenly blush?

She stepped toward him, so close he could almost touch her. Micah's hands longed to close the gap between them, but they were standing on the street, right before his parents' house. He was not fool enough to act indecently here.

"I am, aren't I?" Catherine breathed, gaze lingering on his lips. "Impressive, I mean."

Micah swallowed. *How did she do it?* How did she suddenly transform an innocently spoken phrase like that, make it so erotic he hardly knew what to do with himself?

No, that was not quite right. He knew precisely what he wanted to do.

"Come on," he murmured darkly, taking her hand.

Catherine did not ask any questions as Micah pulled her into the hallway of the de Petras house. There was still arguing going on in the parlor, voices mingling and rising, as he pulled his mistress up the stairs toward the bedchamber he had occupied when a young boy.

The bed within was small, but that did not matter. It was not sleep he had on his mind.

Micah stepped toward the bed, only one thing on his mind, and made to push Catherine onto it, but she evidently had other ideas. Fingers swift on the buttons of his breeches, Micah moaned as she pulled them down, then pushed him onto the bed.

"You'll have to be quiet," she warned, mischief in her eyes as she pulled up her skirts to mount him.

"I can if you can," Micah whispered.

It was not quite true. As she slowly lowered herself onto his manhood, Micah threw back his head and bit his lip, trying desperately not to cry out with pleasure at the intensity of her closeness.

God, she was warm and wet and welcoming, and all he wanted was—

"Catherine," he breathed.

Micah looked up and saw the same expression of delight, of controlled furious passion on her face, and gave himself up to her.

She rode him hard, biting her own lip as her body quivered, and when Micah exploded, pouring himself into her, she collapsed into his arms with little moans of ecstasy that almost made Micah believe he could go again.

Gasping for breath, his entire body tingling with pleasure, Micah smiled as he lay back on the bed. That was precisely what he needed. She really was very impressive.

He tried to shift Catherine aside, but she clung to him. For a moment, Micah thought she wished to stay in his arms for an embrace—a moment of intimacy they rarely bothered with. It was most unaccountable.

Then he remembered how narrow the bed was. Ah, that would be it.

Instead of forcing her off him, Micah twisted, turning to get up off the bed. "I'll have to go back downstairs," he said ruefully. "They'll miss me before long."

He had no wish to go and was gratified to see the same disappointment in her eyes.

"Must you?"

Truly, she was a mistress like no other. Feeling disappointed for him that he would have to spend more time with his family, during a debate like this!

No other mistress was quite so feeling.

"Thank you," said Micah quietly as he buttoned up his breeches. "I needed that release."

"Any time," said Catherine dryly. "I suppose I will see you on Thursday, as ever?"

Micah nodded, then realized what it was Catherine was expecting.

Of course. This was an additional encounter, one beyond their agreement. He had not asked beforehand, though it was clear she had been just as eager as he was…

Still. It was more than they had bargained for, and everyone had a price.

"Here," Micah said, pulling out his pocketbook and retrieving a ten-pound note.

Catherine looked at it for a moment before taking it. In that infinitesimal moment, something strange crossed her face. Micah only saw it for a fraction of a second, but it had definitely been there.

Anger, frustration, and desperation.

It did not make sense, but before Micah could consider it, it was gone.

"Thank you," Catherine said quietly, taking the money and placing it inside her corset.

Micah nodded. "You can sneak out the back way."

She nodded but said nothing.

But he could not worry about that. He had his family to deal with. Sighing heavily, Micah said, "By God, Catherine. I wish I had you with me all the time. It would make my family far easier to deal with."

CHAPTER SIX

September 24, 1812

CATHERINE CLUNG TO Micah's shoulders as their lovemaking gained pace, closer and closer, and—

"Micah!" she cried.

She had told herself she would not cry out his name.

It was too intimate, too close. Too much. Too revealing of her own heart, her mind.

Not that Micah appeared to have noticed, however. Thrusting into her with a groan and falling onto the bed beside her, Micah appeared to have nothing on his mind except their lovemaking. The passion, the connection, the pleasure, the feelings of ecstasy which came in a moment and lingered, delightfully, across the skin.

Catherine tried to get her breath back, but it was difficult when such sensual decadence still endured in her bones.

Try as she might, Catherine could not stop herself from looking over at him. Handsome in that irritatingly chiseled way, entirely opposite to so many of the popinjays who strutted about town.

Micah did not attempt to be handsome. He just was. He was infuriating.

And worst of all, Catherine thought wretchedly, despite her

best efforts, Micah still did not seem to look on her as anything but a rather convenient...release. Was that how he had put it?

"Thank you. I needed that release."

She closed her eyes for a moment, as though that would help her get her bearings, but all it did was transport her back to that memory.

She had known he would be feeling lost and irritated after his visit to his family. They did not appear to be bad people, at least from the stories Micah had told and the little gossip Catherine had heard about the place.

Unusual, perhaps. But not bad people.

And she had been right. When Catherine had been waiting for him, she had seen him emerge, half dazed, from the front door and she had done the first thing that had come to mind. She had seduced him, of course.

Catherine opened her eyes as she smiled ruefully. Not that he would know it, of course. That was the trouble with men—all men, not just Micah.

Always so convinced he was the one making the decisions.

She made sure not to laugh, not while he was lying beside her on her sumptuous bed. No, she had seduced him, ridden him hard and fast, catching her own pleasure as she bestowed it, and he...he saw her as nothing but a release.

Micah had his hand behind his head, a lazy smile on his face.

Instinct took over, as it so often did. Well, it was difficult to prevent it, whenever one was around Micah for more than ten minutes.

Knowing precisely what reception she would be given, Catherine turned into Micah's side, putting an arm over his chest. That was all she wanted, to be held. To snuggle up into him, as though they were a married couple, as if they loved each other, and—

"I have to go," said Micah, turning away and sitting on the edge of the bed.

Catherine swallowed. *Determination was the key, that was all.*

True, she had not convinced Micah to fall in love with her and declare himself yet. But she would. Eventually.

All she had to do was be patient and determined.

"You do know your family is fully aware that you have mistresses, don't you?" she said lightly, pulling the bed cover up over her body—though ensuring it stopped just under her breasts.

Well. She had to tempt him somehow.

Micah snorted with a lopsided grin. "Aware? Did I ever tell you I took Annie as my guest to Emerald's wedding?"

Catherine's eyes widened and red-hot jealousy roared through her heart. "Annie?"

He nodded, as though he had not heard her vicious jealousy. "Yes, I thought her the best—the best to annoy my parents, I mean. In truth, I did not think much about Emerald, though it all worked out for the best, she did not even come."

"Not—your sister jilted her betrothed?" Catherine stared. *The more she heard about this family...* "But I thought she was married."

"Oh, she is, they eloped as it turned out," Micah said easily, pulling his shirt toward him. "I should have expected it, really. Emerald hates attention."

"Unlike you," Catherine teased.

He laughed. "Well, I certainly like the attention you bestow on me."

Micah pulled his shirt over his head just before Catherine had reached out and touched his back.

She withdrew her hand. *Too late.* She had hoped, perhaps, that her touch would be enough to tempt him to stay. To renew their ardor, to return to bed. To return to her arms—

"You don't have to go."

Catherine swallowed and bit her lip. She had not intended to speak aloud. The thought had crossed her mind, sharp and powerful, and had just...slipped out.

Micah did not appear to have heard. "Have you seen my breeches?"

Tempted as she was to merely lie and say she had not, Catherine knew it would do her no good in the end. Micah had decided to leave, and that was what he was going to do. It was getting rarer and rarer, in truth, that he would fall asleep by her side, leaving her in the early hours to awake alone.

Catherine did not know what was worse. Him leaving now and depriving her of that intimate moment as they fell asleep together in the same bed…or waking to find herself alone, without the man she loved.

Not *loved*. Not really.

She retrieved the breeches from the bed, hidden just under the cover she had moved. "I said, you don't have to go. Your family always frustrates you, why not stay here?"

Well, she had said it now, hadn't she? She may as well get a response.

But Micah's laugh was not what she had expected. "Oh, I'm not going to my parents."

And with that, without saying another word, he rose and started to pull on his breeches.

Catherine propped herself up in bed. *Not going to his parents?* Then why on earth was the man so eager to leave her?

It was late—far too late for any man, no matter how impressive his talents, to win much at a gaming table. At least, for most men. So why did Micah wish to leave her?

A strange painful pang entered her heart, and Catherine found her chest constricting painfully. Oh, if she could make it hard for him to leave her…

"Where are you going, then?" she asked, trying as hard as she could to keep her petulance from her voice.

Micah winked. "Back to my lodgings."

Catherine stared as Micah wandered about her boudoir, looking for the rest of his clothes. They had been rather exuberant in their lovemaking. It looked like a whirlwind had torn up the place.

She could not help but smile. Those cries of ecstasy…

Then her mind sharpened. "Back to your lodgings?"

It was most unlike him. Leave her, her warmth, her intimacy, her ability to make him cry out in pleasure, just to go back to his lodgings? That was not the Micah she knew.

Leave her for a more impressive dinner, or a familial obligation, or a planned night gambling with his friends, yes. But to merely go back and sit in his lodgings alone?

Catherine's stomach twisted most horribly. *Unless, of course, he did not plan to be in his lodgings alone.*

It was an unpleasant thought, but one that should have occurred to her immediately. Of course, Micah was not about to leave her to spend the evening alone. Why, a woman was surely scheduled to meet him there. Another woman. A woman he would bed with perhaps the same exuberance and delight as he had just bedded her.

Catherine discovered, quite to her surprise, that her fingers were gripping the bed linens so tightly, she had started to pull it off the mattress.

Micah and another woman.

It was a terrible thought...but not an impossible one. Micah guarded his heart far too well to see any impropriety in the plan.

Before she knew it, Catherine's heart had slipped out onto her tongue. "You don't care about me, Micah."

Micah halted. He was almost completely dressed, and as he straightened up, Catherine could see that only his cravat and jacket were yet to be replaced on his person. There was something so alluring about the way she could see his throat descend into his shirt without the obstruction of a cravat. Something intimate. Something delightful.

"Catherine Tetlow," said Micah, looking a little affronted. "What a thing to say. I do care about you."

But she could see it was merely the patter of a gentleman who wishes to seek calm and peace in his life, rather than someone who actually meant it.

Oh, he meant it, but as a woman might say she cared about a friend's child. In theory, yes, just as long as there was no practical need to do anything about it.

"Yes, you do care about me," said Catherine quietly, feeling a strange sense of boldness overcome her. *This was it. This was the moment.* "But not like that."

"Like that?"

He had taken a step toward her now, and Catherine's heartbeat spiked painfully as he did so. If only he could see her how she wanted, if only his heart skipped a beat like hers!

"You don't care for me," Catherine said, meeting his daring eye. "You want me. You desire me."

Micah frowned. "What's the difference?"

Catherine knew that she could go in one of two directions now, and her choice would seal her fate with the handsome de Petras son.

Either she could laugh it off; tell him she was teasing, that he was so quick to fall for her jokes, and that he would be late for whoever it was he was planning to meet later if he was not careful. A lighthearted way to escape this conversation.

That, or…

Catherine took a deep breath and forced herself to release the bed linens. Or she could reveal her heart. She could own that the arrangement they had started two years ago could simply no longer continue. Not unless…unless things changed. Unless his heart changed.

There would be no going back once these words were said, they could never be unsaid. Catherine knew if she was bold, she would be taking a risk she may regret in a moment.

But was that not what love was?

Catherine swallowed. *How long had she tried to convince herself it was not love?* How long had she told herself love was far too strong a word, that falling in love with Micah de Petras would not only be foolish, but pointless?

But it did not matter. She could not argue away the stars.

"I think that though you do not care for me now, I…I could make you care for me."

Catherine could hardly breathe. *There. The words were said.*

Though they did not echo around the room, they certainly echoed around her heart. Had she chosen the right words? Had she spoken with enough boldness, had her eyebrow been arched enough?

Micah stared, then grinned uncertainly. "I am not quite sure I understand you."

It was a route of escape...but Catherine did not take it. She couldn't, not now. She was absolutely determined to have him.

"I," she said with a winning smile, "will make you fall in love with me."

Silence fell between them for a moment—a silence that made Catherine's heart beat faster. Then—

Micah guffawed. "Make me fall in love—Cat, darling—"

"Don't you Cat darling me," she said warningly.

"But fall in love? Cat, you know I don't have a loving bone in my body," said Micah, still laughing.

Catherine's stomach twisted. She did, or at least, she knew there was no loving bone in Micah's body at the moment, other than the obvious manhood that made love to her every Thursday.

But there was something in him, wasn't there? Something deeper, something she saw in rare moments when he came to her, upset about his family, bruised by their treatment.

Something in him craved a deeper connection. She would find it, she would draw it out—whether he liked it or not.

"I will make you fall in love with me," she repeated, not taking her eyes from him.

Micah's laugh died away as he saw the seriousness in her eyes. "Cat, I am sorry to say that I can guarantee you cannot."

Catherine swallowed. Well, it was painful for Micah to state so easily, categorically, that she would fail. She hadn't even tried yet, he did not know what she would be willing to do, how much she would pour her own heart into the endeavor.

But there was no way to entice Micah, she knew. Except...

"I'd put a wager on it."

Micah had turned away in a fruitless hunt for his cravat, but he turned around immediately to stare, mouth slightly agape.

Catherine smiled, trying to put all her sensuality, all her winning charm into the smile. "That's right. I'll wager you."

"B-But…a wager?" repeated Micah, seemingly unsure whether he had heard her correctly.

Catherine nodded, her heart contracting painfully as she saw his immediate interest. *Was that all it took?* The threat of a gamble, the opportunity to lose money? He had no interest in actually loving her?

"A wager," she repeated. "A wager you clearly think you can win."

That was it, teasing in her air, that delicate way she had of stroking his ego. Catherine saw the impact almost immediately as a smile crept across Micah's face, that satisfied one she saw so rarely, when he was absolutely certain he would win an argument.

"Well now, that is a far more interesting proposition," said Micah, moving to the bed and sitting beside her.

Catherine's breath caught in her throat. He was so handsome, so charming—and so good. Underneath all the bluster, all the charm, was a man who just desperately wished to be loved and accepted. Why could he not accept her love?

"Indeed," she managed to say almost calmly.

"What are your terms?"

"Terms?" Catherine said, feeling herself drawn—as usual—toward him. They were only a few inches apart, and though he was almost entirely clothed, she was naked. Perhaps he would—

"Yes, terms," said Micah, almost impatiently. "What happens if I win, what happens if you win, that sort of thing. Terms?"

Catherine stared for a moment, mind whirling. She had not actually thought this far ahead, had not actually expected him to be so eager for the wager.

If she'd known, she would have spent far more time considering precisely how she could force the man to adore her. As it was, she would need to think quickly.

"Terms," she repeated, keeping her voice level and ensuring that she smiled. "Yes, terms. Well, it's remarkably simple. The aim is to make you fall in love with me—"

"Something that will never happen," Micah cut in with a grin.

"—and if I succeed, which I will," Catherine continued, her own smile no less firm, "then you…you will give me one hundred pounds."

Her heart skipped a beat at the words but they were said now. One hundred pounds! Why, it would care for John and Mary for almost six months. It would be a remarkable coup, a chance to catch her breath, an opportunity to think and plan for their future rather than just exist month to month.

And it would come with Micah's heart, of course…

"It's so unlikely, I am more than happy to agree to such a sum," said Micah, cutting through her thoughts. "But what if you cannot? Make me love you, I mean."

Hearing those words on his lips was painful, but Catherine persevered. *There was too much at stake here. Too much.*

As elegantly and nonchalantly as she could muster, she shrugged. "Then I have lost."

Micah laughed. "Lost? Is that to be your forfeit?"

"What else is there?"

"Don't you think it would be fairer if you were similarly penalized?" teased Micah. "I mean to say, don't you think you should have to give me one hundred pounds?"

Blast. Catherine had not thought of that; her heart wended so close to Micah, the idea of gaining money was merely a bonus to the whole endeavor. If she had him, what need she for money, really?

Besides, it was not as though she had one hundred pounds laying around to give the gentleman. It would be rather galling, in truth, to lose Micah's heart and pay for the privilege.

"No, I don't think so," Catherine said, allowing the bed linens to slip a little more.

Micah's gaze flickered to her breasts, then resolutely returned to her eyes.

Catherine's smile became mischievous. "You are the real prize, Micah. Can't you see that? If I cannot have you, if I am unable to woo you, win you, make you fall in love with me…well, I have lost more than money. I have lost everything."

It was perhaps the most vulnerable she had ever been. It felt wrong, somehow, to admit to this before they had even started, before the wager had been agreed upon, but Catherine knew there was nothing else she could say. Nothing but the truth.

Micah was hesitating. Evidently, he was unconvinced as to the fairness of the scheme, but she could see his natural tendencies to gamble starting to rise.

He wanted to take on the bet; he was so confident, so cocksure his heart would never be in question, it appeared he saw no possibility of losing.

But it was one-sided, and a strange thing to gamble in the first place. Catherine watched the indecision flood across his face, his gaze drifting into the middle distance as he attempted to consider just how he would pull it off.

Catherine held her breath. *This was it.* The moment that decided her fate. Her life would go one way or the other, and it all came down to this moment: to a decision made by a gentleman who was absolutely convinced, to the point of one hundred pounds, that he would never care for her more than he did now.

She would have been offended if she was not so eager to prove him wrong.

Then Micah's gaze sharpened. He grinned, holding out a hand. "It's a wager."

CHAPTER SEVEN

September 30, 1812

"I DON'T KNOW why I have to—"

"Because I have asked you to, that is why," came Opal's stern response.

And that, apparently, was the end of the matter. Oh, Micah knew he could open his mouth and argue, but where would that get him? Absolutely nowhere, it appeared.

So instead of arguing, Micah sighed heavily and leaned against the wall in the hall. "Fine."

"Thank you," his mother said pertly, as though she had not had to spend time convincing her son. "How very kind of you."

Micah rolled his eyes. This was why he had told himself he would not be dropping by the de Petras family home too often, but then he had left his riding boots here quite accidentally, and after being invited by James for a ride in Hyde Park, he'd had no choice.

A short visit, that was what he had told himself. And here he was, almost an hour later, getting roped into *babysitting*.

"It is not babysitting!" Opal had said, wide-eyed when he had pointed this out.

Micah had snorted then, and he snorted now at the very memory. *Not babysitting?* What did they call it then, when he was forced to act as chaperone for a woman who—

"Do you think I look dashing?" beamed Sapphire, half walking, half running down the stairs with a bonnet covered in ribbons held before her.

Micah had to smile. Well, if he was going to be babysitting, he would much rather do it for Sapphire than either of his two nieces. At least Sapphire knew how to conduct herself in polite Society. Mostly.

"It looks hideous," he said calmly.

Sapphire's eyes widened. "I am not hideous!"

"I did not—"

"Micah, what a thing to say to your sister!" came their mother's voice from the parlor.

"That is not what I said! I said the bonnet—where did you get such a monstrous thing, Sapphy?"

Sapphire grinned. "Where do you think?"

Micah shook his head. Mr. Rivers, the haberdasher, had much to answer for. "You cannot truly tell me he willingly sold you such a thing?"

His sister looked at the bonnet in her hands. "I altered it as soon as I got home. See, I added these ribbons, and this lace, and this feather here was quite easy to sew into—"

"I don't need a stitch by stitch account, Sapphy," interrupted Micah with a dry laugh. "Come on. The sooner we get to Hyde Park, the sooner we can leave."

"Oh, no, I want to stay there a good hour and see all the gentlemen walking up and down looking at the ladies looking at them," said Sapphire happily, handing the bonnet to Micah and turning around without another word.

Micah smiled as he carefully placed the bonnet over his sister's riot of curls, and as she turned back to face him, carefully knotted the ribbons in a bow.

It was the one thing Sapphire was unable to do herself. His sister had never let the lack of one hand defy her, nor define her.

"Come on!" Sapphire giggled as she looked up at her brother.

"You never know, even a curmudgeon like you might spot someone you like."

"Sapphire!"

"Don't let her talk to any gentlemen, Micah," came Opal's voice, once again from the parlor. "She may be out, but she is a terrible flirt."

"Mama!" Sapphire stared in horror at the door where their mother was quite clearly listening to their conversation.

Micah grinned. "That she is, Mama. I'll take care of you, don't you worry."

And he meant it. There was something refreshing about being given something to do, an actual task he could complete. As he and his sister stepped out onto the street, bustling as it always was at this time of year when more and more people came from the country to Town, Micah felt a strange sort of contentment settle in his chest.

He had a job to do, take Sapphire to Hyde Park, keep men away, then return her. It was easy, it was simple, it was most certainly not arduous…and though it was a strange thing to admit, even to himself, it was nice to do something for the family. Nice to be asked.

Besides, Sapphire wasn't that bad, as sisters went.

She stuck her arm through his and grinned. "How many gentlemen's cards do you think I should take home for Mama. Fifty?"

Micah chuckled as they started walking. "You are incorrigible, Sapphy."

"Probably," she said lightly, beaming at everyone they passed, her spirit utterly buoyant. "And don't pretend you don't enjoy this, I know you think me your favorite sister."

It was not something Micah would ever admit, even if it was true. Coral was *Coral*, and Emerald was so shy it was difficult to get a clear read of her personality.

So yes, Micah supposed Sapphire was his favorite sister.

"Nonsense," he said aloud. "I love all my sisters equally."

Sapphire rolled her eyes as they turned a corner onto Achilles Way. "Of course you do. That's why you and Coral haven't exchanged a kind word in over a year."

"We have exchanged a—"

"No, you haven't," said Sapphire firmly. "I may be nine years younger than you, Micah, but that does not make me a fool."

Micah had no chance to reply to this outrageous suggestion— even if it was true—because at that moment, they stepped through the gate into Hyde Park and his sister's attention was entirely taken up with something far more interesting than brothers.

"Look! Is that the Duke of Axwick? And the Earl of Clarcton over there, walking with a lady I do not recognize, how interesting—and there's Viscount Shardlow! Oh, Micah!"

"They are not here on display for you," Micah hissed, pulling his sister back as Sapphire attempted to walk toward the people she was so clearly interested in. "Have a little decorum, Sapphy!"

"Decorum is for dull people," Sapphire said with a grin. "Come on, let's go this way!"

Resigning himself to the fact that his sister was going to make an absolute fool of herself, and him in the bargain, Micah allowed himself to be pulled along down a path toward the most interesting of characters in the park.

Not that it mattered. Micah had little interest in meeting with the great and the good of the *ton;* those who were good were usually dreadfully dull conversationalists.

Sapphire sighed happily as they passed the Serpentine lake. "Is it not a beautiful afternoon?"

"If you think so."

His sister groaned, tugging his arm in reproof. "You are miserable today, you know that?"

A twinge of irritation, despite his affection for his sister, gathered in his gut. "I am not miserable—"

"If I say you are, you are," said Sapphire resolutely. "What's going on in that mind of yours? Are you worried about your marriage?"

"My—marriage?" Micah spluttered. *The very idea!* "Sapphire, I have no need to marry!"

She laughed, and he glanced around for a moment to see whether anyone had heard them. Hyde Park was busy, with gentlemen and ladies in large groups and individually walking about the place, hoping to see and be seen…but hopefully not to overhear.

Sapphire was still laughing. "Oh, Micah, you are daft! No one *needs* to marry, you do it because you like someone."

Sometimes, Micah felt as though he and his youngest sister were the same…then she came out with something like that.

No one needs to marry.

Well, he supposed he should be glad Sapphire had grown up in the de Petras family believing that. It was a wonderful idea, the thought that everyone could marry for love, no bargains made between families, no desperate daughters married without dowries, no titled gentlemen wedding fortunes to maintain manors.

In Sapphire's world, it seemed, only true love brought two people together in church.

Micah almost snorted at the thought but managed to contain himself. It was a blessing, really, that Sapphire could believe it. He would not be the one to disillusion her. Not yet, at least.

"Honestly, I cannot think of a single woman I like enough to marry," he said aloud, hoping to change the subject. "So, there's an end to it."

Sapphire glanced up, nose scrunched up in disbelief. "No one? None of your mistresses?"

Catherine. Her face darted into his mind, her delicious body soared into his senses, and Micah almost stumbled as the thought of Catherine overwhelmed him, dulling his awareness of what was around him.

And then he righted himself, forced away the thought of Catherine, and cleared his throat as though he had said something foolish.

Where had that come from?

"I will make you fall in love with me."

Micah almost smiled. Catherine Tetlow. She was a tease, indeed, and in a way she was his favorite mistress. She was certainly the one he had kept the longest, the woman he saw most frequently. The only woman, now he came to think of it, he'd bedded in his family home.

But that did not mean love, and marriage, and all that. Out of the question.

"Who were you thinking of, just then?"

Micah looked awkwardly at his sister, her arm still tucked in his. "Thinking of?"

Sapphire nodded, her face serious. "Your expression was...well, strange. As though you were thinking of someone you truly cared for, and I can tell you now, it wasn't one of us."

Micah swallowed as they passed a gaggle of laughing gentlemen. "I wasn't thinking of anyone in part—"

"Good Lord, a cripple!"

Micah froze, halting in his steps, rage pouring through his veins. The sound had come from one of the men they had just passed, though which one, it was impossible to tell.

"Let's keep going," Sapphire whispered, cheeks scarlet. "Micah, it doesn't matter—"

"And that can't be her husband, no man alive would touch—"

"Say that again and I will run you through with a blade!" roared Micah, releasing Sapphire and stepping toward the brigands.

That anyone would think, much less say such disgusting, such evil—

"Micah, no!"

Someone had a hold of his arm, but it did not matter, Micah was stronger, and he was slowly advancing on the men, some of whom were still laughing, others looking discomforted.

"Who said it?" Micah shouted, blood pounding. "Which one

of you cads have no honor, no respect for—"

"She's only a cripple," one of them said, a pasty-faced little man with a teasing air. "Surely she is not worth—"

Micah's free hand swung, even though it was his left, and punched the man squarely on the nose.

He went down as though struck by lightning, roars of shock from his friends exploding around them, but Micah did not care. His chest was heaving, rage still throbbing in his heart, and he wanted to punch the man again and again until he stayed down and did not—

"Micah, stop it!"

It must be Sapphire who was holding onto his right arm, trying to pull him back, but Micah was far too strong.

"Dear Lord!"

"What's going on there?"

"A brawl! Surely not a brawl!"

"Micah!"

The last voice was different. So much wrath was pouring through Micah's veins he could barely see, let alone hear, but while the chattering voices rose in outrage and laughter around him, one was completely different.

"Micah de Petras, let me handle this!"

Cat. Catherine Tetlow. Micah blinked, it could not be her, he must be dreaming, his fury at the blaggard now lying in a crumpled heap before him must have addled his mind.

But no, there was no mistaking that blonde hair, those red lips—lips usually curled in a smile. He had never seen them in such a thin line before, eyes flashing as she reached the men.

"Mr. Paston, I am ashamed of you," Catherine said haughtily as she halted before them, her gaze as furious as Micah's felt. "Saying such things about a lady in public, while her brother accompanies her! Have you no shame?"

The man, Mr. Paston, if that's what she called him, groaned on the ground.

One of his companions said, "She's only a—"

"She's only a young lady with thoughts and feelings like yours, though I hesitate to say it," snapped Catherine. "Thoughts and feelings far finer than yours, I would warrant, and a mind far superior. What were you, dragged up rather than raised, to say such things?"

A few of the gentlemen were quietly peeling away from the group, Micah noticed, evidently unwilling to be caught up in such a furor, and well they might.

He had never seen Catherine like this. She dominated the group despite being outnumbered six, seven, eight to one. She stood proud, elegant, utterly in control. It was intoxicating. No wonder none of them looked away. Micah could not drag away his own gaze.

"And you, Mr. Ransome, I would have thought you would have far too much riding on your engagement with Miss Loughton to be so scandalous," Catherine said pointedly at a gentleman whose ears were pinking. "And young Mr. Rivers, I do not believe your father would appreciate you bringing his name into disrepute!"

"I didn't say anything to—"

"If you laughed, you are complicit," said Catherine sharply. "Now go, all of you. You are not welcome in Hyde Park."

For a moment, Micah was certain that they would defy her. What was she, after all, but a woman who had appeared out of nowhere? Who was she to forbid them entrance to Hyde Park?

But for some reason, he could not understand, they…obeyed. One by one, the men disappeared, slinking off toward one of the gates.

But there were still murmurs. A crowd had gathered. *Of course it had*, Micah thought wearily. It was too much to hope they would be able to have their own private mortification, they had to suffer the watching gazes of half of the *ton*. At least Sapphire would—

Sapphire.

Micah turned to look for his sister, who was no longer hanging onto his arm. She was standing just a few paces behind him, cheeks still scarlet, stub pulled under her other arm, as though that would make the taunts disappear.

His jaw tightened. It had been a mistake, coming here—but why shouldn't Sapphire de Petras, daughter of a lady, a lady herself, walk one autumnal afternoon in Hyde Park?

"Sapphy?"

Sapphire raised her gaze to meet his, and Micah's heart broke to see unshed tears glistening in her eyes.

The bastards.

"Miss de Petras, are you quite well?" came Catherine's gentle voice.

Sapphire nodded, seemingly unable to speak.

Micah glanced at Catherine. Where she had come from, how she had managed to immediately transform the situation from one of violence to one of berating peace, he did not know. But he was grateful.

"I must say what a delight it is to finally meet you, Miss de Petras," said Catherine lightly, but with just a hint of warmth in her tones. "I have heard such good reports of you, I am honored to find the reports did not do you justice."

Micah watched, astonished, as a small smile crept across Sapphire's lips.

"Truly?"

"There are few sisters who would be capable enough to hold onto their brother's arm in such a bold fashion," said Catherine wryly, glancing at Micah for just a moment. "Come, Miss de Petras, walk with me if you will. My name is Catherine Tetlow."

"A pleasure to make your acquaintance, Miss Tetlow," said Sapphire quietly.

The two women walked side by side, slowly along the path, ignoring Micah, who assumed he was required merely to follow.

So follow he did. Catherine spoke quietly to Sapphire, keeping all her attention, and within a few minutes, Micah watched in astonishment as his sister was drawn out of herself again.

Before long, the two women were laughing away at a jest Sapphire had just made, her composure entirely returned.

Micah could do nothing but marvel. *How had she done it?* What sort of power did she have that he had perhaps never noticed?

Just once Catherine glanced back with a teasing smile.

Micah's stomach lurched.

"I will make you fall in love with me."

"Cat, I am sorry to say that I can guarantee you cannot."

Well, he had not accounted for anything like this, had he? Catherine was not the sort of woman to use a situation like this for her own advantage. Her care of his sister was genuine, and that was what made it all the more potent.

Anyone who could comfort Sapphire like that was special, at least in his books.

"—how do you know my brother?"

Micah's stomach lurched. Sapphire's question was innocently asked, of course, and in most cases it would not matter. But the absolute last thing he needed was—

"Your brother is friends with mine," lied Catherine smoothly. "I have learned to trust him, and he has shared much about your family."

Relief swept through Micah's heart. It was well done; a clever idea that, to pretend they had a prior connection. Yes, his family knew he had mistresses, and yes, he had made the rather unfortunate decision, in hindsight, to bring one of them to what they had thought was Emerald's wedding.

But in this moment, he was not sure whether Sapphire needed to know her rescuer was being bedded weekly by her brother.

"Lord, so you know all about us then," said Sapphire happily. "Who do you think Micah should marry?"

Micah spluttered, "S-Sapphire, there is no need to—"

"What an interesting question, Miss de Petras," said Catherine, casting an amused look over her shoulder before returning to his sister. "You know, I am of the opinion that—"

"James," said Micah gratefully.

James Gresley, the Earl of Maltravers, was striding toward them with a serious look on his face that told Micah he had somehow been informed of the altercation. Amethyst was by his side, having to almost run to keep up.

Damnation. Why was it so difficult to keep anything quiet in London?

"Maltravers!" Sapphire stopped and smiled, seemingly delighted to see their old friend. "Amethyst, what a—Miss Tetlow, are you acquainted with—"

"I've come to tell you that you must come home, Sapphy," said James breathlessly.

Micah's breath caught in his throat. "My parents?"

"All is well, except—well, they heard about..." James smiled awkwardly, evidently unsure of Catherine.

"Come on, Sapphire," said Amethyst in a low voice. "I think it is better if we—"

"They want you home, Sapphy," said James in an undertone. "Now."

Micah's heart sank heavily like a stone. *Of course they had already heard, and of course they wanted Sapphire home as soon as possible.* They had trusted their youngest, most vulnerable daughter to him, and he had not cared for her sufficiently.

It was galling, in truth, to be such a disappointment to his parents.

All he'd had to do was protect her, and he hadn't even managed to do that.

Sapphire sighed heavily. "I don't suppose I could argue with—"

"If you would like to argue with your mother, you are a braver soul than I," said James with a wry laugh. "Come on, Sapphire. Micah, are you coming with us?"

Micah glanced at Catherine. He should return to his parents, really, explain what happened. Give an account of himself, convince them he had done nothing wrong. That would be the correct thing to do.

"No," he said, still not looking away from Catherine. "No, I should ensure Miss Tetlow is returned home safely. There…there may still be ruffians in the place."

James nodded as though that was a perfectly reasonable excuse. For all Micah knew, it was. He could hardly think straight, not anymore. Not with Catherine's intoxicating and continuously intriguing presence before him.

"Micah," said Sapphire quietly as Amethyst pulled her away. "Micah, you did nothing wrong—"

"Go with James, Sapphy," said Micah, interrupting what he knew would be a speech full of pity. A speech he did not want to hear. "And tell Mama…tell Mama."

She nodded. Words were not needed between them.

He watched, wretched as his sister walked off arm in arm with a better man. *Not that it was hard,* Micah thought. Most gentlemen appeared to be better than him.

And Amethyst, too, now that was a surprise. He would not have expected their cousin to be a part of this—but then, his mother could not have made it more clear that he was a disappointment in this regard, could she? Sending a friend of the family and the cousin that just appeared last year.

"You are ashamed of me."

Micah started. Catherine was watching him with a strange look on her face.

"Ashamed?" Micah shook his head as couples passed them by on the path. "Not in the slightest. I am impressed, in truth, with the way that you handled that situation."

"Oh, you break up a few fights, you soon know how to ridicule a man into submission," said Catherine lightly, though there was no laughter in her eyes. "But you are ashamed of me, Micah. You had no wish for your sister to know who I was."

"Of course not!" *What did she think, that he routinely introduced his mistresses to his family?* "You and I, we have an understanding—"

"Yes, we do," cut in Catherine. "Have I made you fall in love with me yet?"

And suddenly all the tension was gone, and Micah laughed weakly as he took her hand in his own. "Not yet."

Her fingers were warm, a tingling creeping across his skin at the contact. God, it was a long time until Thursday…

"You asked if I was ashamed of you, and I can only guess that is because you were watching my face when James…when the Earl of Maltravers…" Micah swallowed. He was not one to admit to things as weak as feelings, but this felt different. "I was ashamed of myself. My temper. My inability to protect my sister."

Catherine squeezed his hand, and when she spoke, her voice was warm. "You did what any brother would do."

"I would have much rather have had you by my side," Micah found himself saying. "You were invaluable, Catherine. I am in your debt."

A strange smile crept across her face, and Micah's stomach churned. It was not a painful sensation, quite to the contrary.

"In truth," Micah said quietly, hardly knowing why he was admitting this, "I was ashamed, but only because…well. You are not the sort of woman a man makes his mistress, are you?"

Catherine raised an eyebrow. "I beg your pardon?"

"You are—are beautiful, and courageous, and quick-witted." Micah's voice was so soft, he hardly knew how she could hear him, but the words flowed from him, unencumbered by thought. "How did I manage to land you as a mistress, Catherine?"

She smiled, her fingers squeezing his, then disappearing. The lack of contact, the break in connection between them was so painful, Micah almost gasped aloud.

"I honestly do not know," she said lightly.

"And I could lose you one day."

Why had the thought never occurred to him? That at any time, Catherine may tire of their arrangement and decide to break it—to break him?

Catherine's red lips curled into a smile. "Well, you know what to do about that, don't you?"

CHAPTER EIGHT

October 5, 1812

S *HE WAS NOT,* Catherine told herself firmly, *going to Hyde Park again merely because she thought Micah may be there.*

Probably not. Almost certainly not.

Which did not explain why the moment she had stepped into the park, Catherine's eyes darted about looking for a certain gentleman.

A couple laughing, children screaming as they ran about, governesses behind them trying to control them, a family riding, a gentleman walking purposefully as though late for an appointment…

But no Micah.

Catherine's shoulders slumped. It was ridiculous. She knew when she was going to see him every week, and Micah had never missed a Thursday yet. There was no reason to go seeking him out.

Except there was every reason.

"I will make you fall in love with me."

Catherine took a deep breath and started to walk down the path as though she had not a care in the world.

She had given herself a rather impressive challenge and felt no closer to winning Micah's heart as she did the horse races. And how would she if she only saw him one evening a week? Why, that was what she had been doing for over two years now, and what good had it done her?

None. She had been unable to tempt Micah's heart to care for her more than a mere mistress, and that meant something had to change. She had to see him more often.

But it was not as though a mistress could turn up at a gentleman's lodgings and demand to see him. Or his club. Or his parents' home.

Catherine almost smiled at the thought of knocking on the door of the de Petras home and requesting to see Micah. She had been bold enough to go there in the first place. She had never met Opal de Petras but did not need to. Her reputation preceded her.

So, she was forced here. Hyde Park. Even though there was no possibility of—

"—damnit, Glaenarm, I just don't see why!"

Catherine blinked. If she did not know any better, she would have said one of the pair of gentlemen ahead of her was Micah de Petras.

It sounded like him. It even looked like him from here, though it was possible she could have mistaken him for someone else. There were only so many styles of coat and breeches that a gentleman could try, after all.

But two things made her pause.

Firstly, the gentleman who could be Micah de Petras looked utterly put out, from what she could tell. Catherine increased her pace, passing an older woman and finding herself just a few paces behind the two men.

It *was* Micah de Petras. Which made the second reason she had assumed it was not him all the more astonishing.

He was pushing a perambulator.

Catherine's stomach lurched. *What did she know of Micah, really?* Only what he told her. Only a few snippets she had managed to glean the rare times she attended anything that also happened to host a person from the *ton.*

She had never heard any whispers of a wife, of a child, but that did not mean…Micah might have hidden that.

"—outrageous," the other gentleman with Micah was saying as they walked sedately along the path. "Just outrageous."

Catherine swallowed, trying to calm her frantically beating heart, but it was getting increasingly difficult to do so.

Did Micah have a wife? Was she truly a mistress in all senses of the word—had he a family she knew nothing of? When Micah had said he had to return to his lodgings, a place she had never been permitted to visit…was that because his wife and child were asleep there?

The thought was repellent, causing bile to rise in her chest. Catherine could not understand it; why lie about that? Why hide the truth?

"I will make you fall in love with me."

It felt hollow now, that wager they had made together. If Micah was already married, was he not in love with his wife?

It was astonishing. It was unbelievable. It was happening right before her eyes, the torment she would never claim Micah's heart, never know what it was to be loved by him—

"—nothing else I could have done, in the circumstances," Micah was saying.

Catherine attempted to hush her frantic thoughts and listen as she walked surreptitiously behind them. What were they talking about? Would she gain an insight into just how Micah could have lied to her for so long about something so important?

"I do not think there was anything else to do, from the story you and Maltravers told," said Micah's companion, sighing heavily. "I mean, the brute! To say such a thing to anyone—but to Sapphire!"

"I would have torn him limb from limb if Sapphy had not been holding onto me," came Micah's reply. "But there it was. I could only punch him once, to my shame."

"Better that than letting him think he could get away with it."

The gentlemen continued talking as Catherine realized what

they were speaking about. The altercation almost a week ago.

At least, unless there was another, more recent occurrence. Catherine shivered. The idea a woman like that, so kind, so clearly gentle, could endure such treatment more than once—it was obscene!

"—took her home," Micah was saying with a sigh as he pushed the perambulator along the path as it curved. "If it hadn't been for Cat—"

"Who?" asked the man curiously.

Heat flushed Catherine's cheeks as she watched the back of Micah's neck redden.

Of course, he would not wish to admit to her, she thought dully. Not now she knew he had a wife and child—at least one child, for there was no knowing how many more there were.

Catherine's heart skipped a beat. *Children with his hair, and his eyes—*

"Oh, just one of my mistresses," said Micah nonchalantly.

It was all Catherine could do to continue walking in silence. *How could he say that?*

Perhaps Micah was not the man she thought he was.

Micah's companion appeared to be of the same opinion. "Come on, man, you cannot just speak of your mistresses as though they were horses!"

"I don't!" Micah protested, though Catherine had to quell a smile. "You asked, and I answered! Here, you take this thing, 'tis far heavier than I thought."

He passed the baby carriage to his friend, and Catherine held back, terrified they would turn and see her walking so closely she could overhear them. But the exchange was made with very little fuss, and the two gentlemen continued walking.

"I don't know why we have to go out with it," said Micah, jerking his head at the perambulator.

Catherine's mouth fell open. *Well, of all the self-centered—*

"It's just a walk," his companion pointed out. "Not very taxing, surely, even for a layabout like you."

Micah nudged him with a dry laugh, and Catherine tried not to look at the way he held himself, the strength in his arms, the powerful confidence emitted from every inch of him.

It was even more painful now, now that she knew him married with children. To think if she had been bolder before, she might have...but for all she knew, Micah had been married when they had first met. Perhaps there had never been any chance of claiming his heart.

"Yes, I know it's just a walk," Micah was saying. "But it's a walk with a baby."

He pointed at the babe, and Catherine could not help but look.

It was a girl, at least as far as she could make out. Soft downy red hair covered the baby's head. She was sleeping.

Though her heart twisted painfully, she was at least relieved to see the baby looked very little like Micah. That, at least, was some relief.

Then her stomach jolted as though she had missed a step while descending stairs. *But that must mean...Lord, that must mean the babe looked like its mother! Micah's wife...*

"You are a duke!" Micah said with a dry laugh. "You should be at court, riding around the countryside, or gambling, something exciting. Don't you get tired of babysitting?"

Catherine's eyes darted to what she could see of the man beside Micah. He was not quite as tall, but with a well featured frame, from what she could tell.

He was also laughing. "Micah de Petras, it is not babysitting, it's parenting! What sort of a father would I be, if I had no desire to spend time with my own child?"

Catherine's heart stopped. It stopped for not one, but several beats as the gentlemen's laughter and conversation continued, and it was only when she forced herself to take a breath that her heart appeared to continue again.

His child—the duke's child! *It was not Micah's baby.*

A wave of relief soared through Catherine in such a rush, she hardly knew what to do with herself. She felt heavy, exhausted, as though she had run several miles in her long skirts.

It was not his baby. There was no reason to suppose, now she came to think about it, that Micah was married, if it was not his child.

Wait…had not Micah told her something about a duke before?

"She is your niece, and you would do well to acclimatize yourself to the idea of having one, now you have two," said the duke cheerfully.

Niece? Catherine tried desperately to think. Sapphire was unmarried, and Emerald had married…but was it to a duke? No, that was Coral, wasn't it? Difficult as it was to keep up with the ever-changing politics of the de Petras family, she was almost sure.

"My nieces are all very well, but they are nieces, not mine," said Micah flatly. "And if you ask me—oh, blast."

Catherine stifled another laugh. The way Micah spoke, it was as though the world had ended, but the only reason he had stopped speaking was—

"Oh, Amber, don't cry," said Micah's brother-in-law, hastily pausing his steps and peering into the perambulator. "Your mother will think I don't take care of you!"

"You don't."

"Shut up, Micah."

Catherine halted, ensuring she was not too close to the gentlemen or the carriage, from which erupted a scream the like she had never heard, not even when John had been born.

"Make it stop," said Micah in a rush, leaning over the perambulator in turn. "Glaenarm!"

"I don't know how to make it stop, I'm not a mind reader!" said the father hurriedly.

The baby continued to cry, and Catherine had to shake her head. Well, she had thought the worst, and now she knew it to be false; but really, it was almost funnier this way.

To think she had believed Micah a parent! She should have

known better, should have trusted her gut. The way he was talking to it now, as though he had never seen a baby before…

"Please be quiet, Amber," he was murmuring to the screaming infant, as though she merely needed to be reasoned with. "There is no need to cry, your father is here!"

"Come on then, little one," said the duke heavily.

Catherine watched as the father lifted the crying baby, holding her carefully in his arms as he looked in the blankets for something.

"Blast."

"What is it?" Micah said urgently.

It was perhaps her imagination, but if Catherine was not mistaken, there was a large dollop of concern in Micah's tone. He truly cared about the child, no matter what he may say.

Something small and warm sparked in Catherine's heart. It was almost like hope.

Well, if he could be so caring to a child of another…was it not possible that one day, if he was to fall in love with her…well, that perhaps he could—

"Here," said the duke firmly. "Take her."

"Take—Glaenarm!"

Micah's startled cry did not stop his brother-in-law from depositing the baby in his arms.

Catherine watched, entranced, as Micah tried awkwardly both to hold the screaming child and to hand her back to her father. It was almost amusing, though there was a slight concern he may drop her. The man did not seem to have any idea what he was doing, all thumbs.

"I think I've dropped one of her blankets," said the duke airily, as though he frequently offered his child to men who had no idea how to hold one. "I'll only be a moment."

Catherine stepped behind a convenient tree as the man rushed past her, muttering something under his breath about blankets as Micah called out after him.

"Don't leave me alone with her!"

It was certainly not an image of Micah Catherine had ever seen before. From this vantage point, she could see him holding the baby under the arms as she screamed blue murder into his face.

Oh, to see him like this…in such a familial setting, uncomfortable as he clearly was…

It was a view into a world, into a life that Catherine could only dream of.

"My goodness, Micah," she said aloud in a teasing voice, stepping toward the man still awkwardly holding the child. "I did not know you had a baby."

Panic blossomed across Micah's face, so obviously, Catherine laughed. "I don't!"

She looked pointedly at the child still screaming and squirming in his arms. "Really?"

Catherine beamed. All seemed right with the world. Micah was not married, he did not have children, and if she could just be determined enough, she would find herself so much more than merely a mistress.

The panic in Micah's eyes died away as he saw her laughing. "Very funny."

"I thought it was rather amusing," said Catherine lightly. "Go on, hold her properly."

"I don't know how to—"

"Yes, you do," she said without hesitation. "How does your sister hold her?"

Micah looked for a moment as though he would quite like to be rid of the screaming infant, but then looked down at the child.

Catherine looked at her, too. Yes, definitely red hair, though it was fine and would not hold its color until the babe was a little older. Coral's child, it had to be. A de Petras baby.

Ignoring the continued cries, Micah shifted her so she was in the crook of his arm.

As if by magic, the noise stopped. Catherine could hardly remember what Hyde Park sounded like without all that clamor, but now it was gone, a gentle peace descended on the place.

Micah stared, shocked, at the baby who was now calmly blinking up at him, face red and cheeks wet, but otherwise entirely peaceful.

"You're a natural," Catherine said softly.

He cleared his throat awkwardly. "I...well, I am not sure about that. Her father is—"

"A duke, I think you said," she interrupted with a wry laugh. "Which makes this little one Lady Amber."

"Goodness, I had never thought of that," said Micah, smiling briefly up at Catherine before his attention was once more claimed by the quiet child. "Lady Amber. A better title than me before she even starts."

If Catherine had not been listening for it, she probably would not have heard the frustration in Micah's words. But she knew him well, better than he thought.

Oh, he had no real envy of the babe in his arms. It was what she represented that proved to be such a bother, that tugged at his heart. That challenged his place in the world.

"She's pretty."

Micah snorted. "She looks like Coral."

"She must be pretty," said Catherine archly. "No matter how much you dislike her."

"Dislike is a strong word. She's my sister," Micah said firmly, "and I won't hear a word against her."

"Unless you're saying it."

He grinned at that, his eyes gleaming as he caught her gaze. "Yes, I suppose so."

Catherine reached out, unable to help herself. She could still remember when Mary and John had been this small. It was over so quickly, before one even had a chance to notice.

Amber grasped at Catherine's proffered finger and babbled something happily.

"She likes you."

"She's in good company," said Catherine with a laugh. "So

this is Coral's first child?"

Micah nodded. "Emerald has one, and if you ask me, another on the way. The de Petras family continues to expand. I suppose Sapphire will have her own one day."

Catherine nodded, swallowing down the words she wanted to ask but knew she could not. *And would Micah have children one day?* When he found a wife, because he would, if his mother had anything to do with it...would he welcome children into the world, hold them like this, comfort them like this?

An image flashed across her mind, one so startling and so clear it was almost impossible not to gasp.

A child. About three or four years old, with her hair and his eyes, laughing away raucously as Micah swung them around. *Their child.*

"Cat?"

Catherine blinked. The image was gone, replaced by reality; the reality of Micah, a gentleman who did not love her and was determined he would not, holding a child which was not hers. Was not theirs.

"Catherine, are you quite well?" Micah said, a little more concerned. "You looked...well. Strange."

Catherine smiled weakly. What could be gained by admitting to such a hope, such a fantasy? Unless she was able to seduce him, truly seduce him, body and soul, then there was no point allowing her mind to wander in that way.

"Nothing," she said with a smile. "I should leave you. I am sure you have no wish to introduce me as your friend's sister to another of your family."

"Cat—"

But she did not wait. Removing her finger from the tiny yet strong grip of baby Amber, Catherine walked away as the Duke of Glaenarm approached.

She would not cry. She would do better. Next time, Micah would not know what to do with himself in her presence.

CHAPTER NINE

October 11, 1812

"**O**H, MICAH…"

"Yes," murmured Micah, clutching the woman's naked form to him.

On any other day, he would have described her as wonderful. But for some reason—

"Kiss me, Micah," she urged.

Micah obliged, but more out of politeness than anything else.

This was ridiculous! He had come here tonight in the full expectation of bedding the woman, happily and comfortably, then returning back to his rooms for a late supper. Why, he'd even decided on which pie to purchase on the way home, having sampled almost all of them in his unwillingness to keep a servant who could cook.

But here he was, lying in bed with her, pressed up against him, her nipples grazing his chest…and all Micah could do was look at the ceiling.

It was unfathomable. Ridiculous. It was, in truth, worrying. Was he losing his touch?

She moaned. "Micah!"

Micah turned over to push her onto the bed below him, kissed her neck rather matter-of-factly, and she squirmed underneath him.

"Love me!"

Love me. It was a demand Micah was hearing more often now, though Polly's request was entirely different to Catherine's.

"Micah!"

"What?" Micah said hurriedly, looking at Polly's upturned lips. "Oh, yes."

He kissed her again, but broke it off far quicker than he would have and instead of entering her, sinking himself into her and riding her until sweet relief...Micah rolled away.

"Micah?"

He sighed. *It was just...well.* Despite all efforts to the contrary, he had to admit he was simply not interested in bedding Polly tonight.

Which was odd. It was her night, and he never usually had trouble. If anything, it was keeping his manhood down that was the issue, not the other way around.

But despite Polly's best efforts, despite her sensual dance earlier as she removed her clothes, despite the feeling of her pressed up against him...Micah had to admit he was simply not interested in bedding his second mistress.

Strange.

"Micah?" Polly pawed at him nervously. "Are you unwell?"

Unwell? Micah shook his head, though perhaps he was. He could conceive of no other reason why he had no wish to bed the delightful brunette. She was his only other mistress at the moment.

A strange lurch ripped through his stomach as he thought her name. *Catherine.*

"Micah de Petras, are you going to bed me or not?"

Micah ignored her. Perhaps there was something wrong with him. His head had felt heavy, confused, full of thoughts he could not understand for the last few days. Ever since...

The image of Catherine flashed in his mind; elegant, charm-ing, blonde with those teasing smiles that made her eyes sparkle with mischief. Mischief he wanted to join her in…

His manhood twitched.

Damn. It did not make any sense!

Polly pushed herself up. "You sickening for something?"

Micah was half in a mind to say he was, though what precisely he was sickening for, he could not say. It was odd. He was not usually a man to indulge in such fantasies, not when he had a real woman right here, literally begging for his touch… But now the image of Catherine had flickered through his mind, he found himself returning to it.

Wanting to return to her. To Catherine. To her warm and welcoming arms…

"I will make you fall in love with me."

"Cat, I am sorry to say that I can guarantee you cannot."

"You are the real prize, Micah. Can't you see that? If I cannot have you, if I am unable to woo you, win you, make you fall in love with me…well, I have lost more than money. I have lost everything."

Micah sat up in bed.

"Micah!"

"Yes, I know," he said listlessly as Polly tried to kiss his neck.

He pulled away. This was mischief that Catherine had planted in his mind, that was all.

"Where are you going?"

Micah turned to reply to Polly's plaintive cry, and an impulse that came from somewhere within him that he had never known before rose up in his chest.

He wouldn't say it, even though he had thought it. People thought things all the time, but that did not mean they had to say them.

"This arrangement is at an end."

Polly blinked, evidently completely at a loss. "What?"

Micah pulled on his breeches, finding to his utter astonishment that with every step he took away from Polly, the better he felt. "This arrangement. I'm ending it."

"But when will I see you again?" asked Polly, evidently not

understanding a word he was saying.

Sighing, he pulled on his shirt and started doing the buttons. "You won't."

"But—but I don't understand!" Polly sat up properly in the bed, breasts heaving, and Micah found to his distress that he did not care.

Did not care! About breasts?

There was something seriously wrong with him, and it appeared the only way he could cure it was by going to see Catherine. Well, fine, that's what he would do.

Putting aside Polly now, that was another thing entirely. Why had he said that?

Micah could not understand it, but as he pulled his boots on, he felt the rightness of the decision. He had been playing with Polly for a few weeks now, but she did nothing to excite him, nothing to interest him. Her conversation was dull, her opinions bland, and though pretty—

"Have I done something wrong?"

"No," he said aloud. "No, I just—I am ending this arrangement."

"But why?"

"I don't have to give explanations," said Micah tersely. *Really, she was pushing his patience now.* Did she think endless questions would tempt him back? "Explanations are for husbands, not lovers."

"But—"

"Polly," Micah said heavily. "I do not know what to tell you. I just...I can't anymore. I am sorry."

He had no wish to upset her, no wish to hurt her...but no wish to see her again either. All the desire she inspired was gone, though where it had disappeared, Micah could not tell.

"Here's twenty."

Micah placed two ten-pound notes on the console table by the door, and saw a look of relief mingle with Polly's confusion.

It was the money, of course it was. Well, Polly would soon find someone else, and Micah was free of her.

Free of her? Where had that thought come from?

"Goodbye, Polly."

She may have replied; Micah had stepped through the door and onto the street so swiftly, he almost collided with someone walking along the pavement.

"My apologies."

"Watch where y'going," came the uncouth reply.

Micah grinned into the October night air. He was not in the respectable part of town, naturally, so he could not expect any different a reply. But he was free. All the tension in his shoulders was gone.

Not just for the evening, but from Polly.

When had he started to consider her a chain around his neck? Micah could hardly tell, and as he wandered down the pavement in no particular direction, he could not recall a time when the slight affection he had for her started to dissipate.

Recently, probably. A few weeks ago everything had been perfectly fine. Even last week, though he was a little bored, he had been able to finish what he had started.

But he had no appetite for her anymore. That was the truth, and though Polly may not like it, there was naught he could do about it. Which left him only one mistress. Catherine.

Micah looked up in startled surprise to find himself standing outside of Cat's rooms.

How had he got here?

Glancing along the street, it appeared he had managed to navigate around a gaggle of drunk ladies who were trying to tempt him into bed, barely noticing them.

Micah shook his head, as though ridding his ears of water. *What was wrong with him?*

Well, now he was here, there was no reason why he should not go up, even if it wasn't Catherine's day of the week.

A surge of joy rushed through Micah, almost rocking him with its strength and intensity. *Cat.* Being close to her, holding her in his arms—even holding her hand would be comfort now.

Clearing his throat and reminding himself he was not in love with Catherine—or anyone, if it came to that—Micah let himself into Parson's Buildings and walked up the familiar staircase to the third floor where Catherine's rooms could be found. When he approached the door, he at first reached for the handle.

Then he hesitated. This was not his agreed night with Catherine. It was more than likely that she had locked it.

Still, it was rather strange knocking on a door that he had previously only seen as a temporary barrier between himself and a woman he was about to bed.

Micah knocked and waited. And waited.

He knocked again, and called out, "Catherine. Cat, it's me."

Still, there was no response, which was utterly perplexing. *Where was she?*

Micah swallowed, his heart skipping a beat painfully. Now he came to think of it, what did he know of her? What did Catherine do the other six nights of the week when she was not bedding him?

Making a mental note to ask her—he would run no risk of falling in love with her just by asking, after all—Micah knocked again. "Catherine?"

"Catherine, I…"

Micah moved hurriedly away from the door, stepping into the dark shadow at the end of the corridor. He had spoken Catherine's name, yes, but then so had someone else. Someone with a deep voice, like his own.

Certainly not someone he wanted to be saying her name with that soft reverence, that gentle desire he recognized.

Footsteps. Micah watched, hardly able to believe his eyes, as Catherine elegantly rose up the staircase, adorned in a brilliant red satin gown that matched her lips perfectly…with a gentleman by her side.

Revulsion and envy stirred in Micah's stomach as he watched the nameless gentleman say something soft in her ear—becoming rage as Catherine laughed delicately at his words.

The blaggard was attempting to seduce her!

"—cannot possibly allow you in," Catherine was saying in almost a teasing air as she reached the door to her rooms. "You know that, Mr. Lister."

"Ah, but I know no such thing, and I beg you to reconsider," said the slimy man with a laugh, taking her hand in his own. "In fact, I know quite the opposite…"

His voice trailed away meaningfully as Catherine leaned against her door, Mr. Lister leaning closer and closer, his eyes so evidently fixed on her lips, until—

"That's close enough, my man," said Micah as he stepped forward.

Mr. Lister had evidently not been expecting company. "Blast you!"

But Micah had nothing to fear when the man stepped toward him, evidently furious his chance to kiss Catherine had passed. He was strong and in the right.

In the right? Thoughts whirling through his mind did not make sense. In the right? Catherine was not his to protect—so why did he feel such a powerful urge to halt the man in his tracks before he touched her?

"Who are you?" Mr. Lister snapped.

Micah smiled. He was not looking at the irritating man, his gaze was all for Catherine, and he saw with delight just how pleased she was to see him.

And then her smile disappeared as quickly as it had come, as she looked at Mr. Lister.

"My name is immaterial, as is yours," said Micah smoothly. "I think your time with the lady this evening is at an end."

Mr. Lister snorted. "What, so that yours can begin?"

"Please, Mr. Lister, I will see you tomorrow as we have planned."

Micah could hardly believe it. Instead of forcing the cad away, as he had expected, Catherine had placed a soothing hand on his arm. She had actually touched him—actually said she would see him on the morrow!

The irritation in Mr. Lister's eyes disappeared as he turned to her. "Yes. Yes, of course. Well, in that case, until tomorrow, Miss Tetlow."

He bowed as she curtseyed, and Micah fought the temptation to punch him.

Mr. Lister's footsteps echoed down the staircase as Micah stood, staring at Catherine, and he said nothing until the door to the street below opened and closed.

"What in God's name—"

"I did not expect to see you this evening, Micah, or I would have prettied myself," said Catherine nonchalantly, turning away and unlocking her door. "What a pleasant surprise."

She stepped through it, leaving Micah to stare after her, open-mouthed.

What a pleasant surprise!

"What was that godawful man doing here?" he demanded, following her.

Catherine raised an eyebrow as she placed her reticule on a table. "I beg your pardon?"

"You know precisely what I mean! That—that man!" Micah said, pointing a finger at the door. "What did you think you were doing with him?"

Anger as he had never known before was pumping through his veins, red-hot, boiling his mind so it was impossible to think of anything else except the way Catherine had so carefully calmed the blaggard.

Seeing her with another gentleman—it was intolerable.

"You have other mistresses," Catherine pointed out calmly as she sat by the fire.

Micah hesitated, glancing about the room as though that would provide him with a response. He had never spent much time in this room before; he was usually moving as quickly as he could to the boudoir.

It was a sort of drawing room, though the fire had a kettle over it, which suggested it acted as a kitchen, too. It was elegant in a way, yet threadbare and with none of the sophistication his mother, Coral, or Emerald had in their drawing rooms. But it was homely, cared for, evidently loved.

"I do not see the problem."

Micah's attention jerked back to the woman before him. "You don't?"

Catherine shrugged. "You have other mistresses, and I…well. I thought I would interview Mr. Lister, see if he was suitable to become a…companion."

Companion. Micah could almost spit the word, he was so furious.

True, he and Catherine had never agreed to exclusively reserve themselves for each other…and he had spoken with her about his other mistresses.

But that was beside the point. Somehow.

"I don't have any other mistresses."

The words had spilled from his lips before he could stop them, and Micah was rather affronted to see Catherine laugh from her armchair.

"Micah, I am not a fool. You talk about them enough!"

"I have ended things with Polly," said Micah, stepping forward, needing to be close to her. "And she was the only other one. Other than you."

He caught her gaze, and her laughter stopped abruptly. Micah swallowed, hardly knowing what to make of this rather odd moment. It was…something he had never experienced with anyone before.

She was looking at him as though…as though he had done something ridiculous, and wonderful, and glorious.

"You have?"

Micah nodded. "I have something for you."

It was a miracle he had kept the box in his coat pocket all day. It was bizarre, now he came to think of it, as he'd had no plans to see Catherine. But he had picked it up from the jewelers that morning and had seen no reason to leave it in his rooms.

Catherine's eyes widened. "You have?"

Micah stepped forward, perching on the arm of a sofa beside the armchair where Catherine sat. For some reason, his fingers were shaking as he drew out the red velvet box.

There was a very sudden intake of breath. "Micah."

"It's not much," Micah said hastily.

He had never purchased jewelry for a woman before. His mother did not count. He had wanted something different, something that could not be misconstrued as a sign of affection, but at the same time, an expression of his...sentiments.

"A thank you," he added quietly. "For your help with Sapphire those weeks ago."

With slightly trembling fingers, Catherine took the box from his hands and opened it. Her gaze fixed on its contents, while Micah found he could do nothing but look at her. The surprise in her face, the color of her cheeks.

Had he ever seen Catherine blush before? How had he never noticed the delicate color of her cheeks, the way her whole body quivered when anticipating something delightful?

"Earrings," Catherine breathed.

Micah grinned awkwardly. "I know."

She drew them up, a long gold chain carefully wrought around two stones. Two brown, dull stones.

Catherine looked up, a teasing smile on her face. "They're not diamonds."

"I should think not," Micah said wryly. "You think I'm made of money?"

"Then what, you've given me rocks?"

"No!" For some reason Micah could not explain, it was very important to him she understand precisely what he had given her. Why it mattered. Why the gift was...special. "It's micah. See?"

He reached out and pointed at the stone enclosed in the gold setting. Catherine's gaze followed his fingers, and her teasing smile softened as she looked at them.

The micah stones had been hard to find, the jeweler said, but Micah was almost certain he had said that to hike up the price. Still. They looked different than the sort of earrings the ladies of fashionable Society were wearing these days.

"Micah?" breathed Catherine.

He nodded. "A token of my aff—gratitude."

Catherine looked up, placing the earrings back in the box. "Thank you."

He smiled, a warm, calming sensation pooling in his stomach. It was pleasant sitting here with Catherine. Something very different from their usual amorous encounters, but—

"This does not mean I will necessarily stop seeing Mr. Lister."

Micah's temper flared. "I do not want you to—"

"You said you would not fall in love with me," Catherine pointed out, eyebrow raised. "And I made no promises to bed only you, Micah de Petras. Now, tell me. Why do you not wish me to see Mr. Lister?"

Micah opened his mouth, struggled to think of any coherent words that would in any way adequately describe his feelings, and closed it again.

After all, how could he speak about emotions he did not understand? There was a strange sort of possessive rage overtaking his heart, his chest was tight, and—were his fingers tingling? Was that just his imagination?

Whatever it was, it was damned uncomfortable. All because of that damned Mr. Lister.

"I don't want you to see Mr. Lister," Micah said quietly, "and not because I am in love with—I mean, I am not in love with you!"

Now there was a slip of the tongue if ever there was one. Heat flushed Micah's cheeks as he tried not to think about what he had just said. Well, a man could get flustered every once in a while, couldn't he?

Both of Catherine's eyebrows were raised now as she leaned

back in her chair. "You aren't, are you? Are you quite sure of that, Micah?"

He could resist no longer. He had wanted to kiss her since the moment his feet had led him inextricably to Catherine's door.

Pulling her upright so rapidly she dropped the jewelry box, thankfully closed, Micah kissed Catherine hard on the mouth.

She immediately melted into his arms, and Micah could have cried out, it was so glorious. There was only one Catherine, no one else could compare to her—no wonder he had to break things off with Polly. How could he kiss Polly when he could be kissing Catherine? The warmth of her, the sweet taste of her, the way she moaned in his mouth as his hands tightened around her buttocks, drawing her closer—

"Micah," Catherine said.

Micah groaned, unable to stop himself. His tongue darted to her lips, and she welcomed him in, the softness of her breasts pressed against him and the promise of something wonderful to come as Catherine clung to him, eager for more, desperate for—

He pulled away. Releasing Catherine from him, stepping away as his heart beat rapidly, Micah took a deep breath.

"I am sure," he said thickly, not understanding how he was upright but knowing he had to prove a point, even if it would drive his manhood wild. "I am not in love with you, Cat."

She stood just as unsteadily as he felt, blinking in the surprise of his sudden absence.

Micah swallowed, and knew, without a shadow of a doubt, that if he stayed here tonight, he would be in danger of being precisely what he kept stating he was not.

"I must go."

"Go?" Catherine blinked, and she followed him to the door. "Go, why?"

Micah did not reply but instead pressed a piece of paper into her hands.

She glanced down at it and her gaze hardened. "Ten pounds."

"The usual," said Micah with a tight smile.

That was it, he had to remind her, remind himself that this was a business arrangement. He may feel everything when he was with her, but that was all it was. Business.

Catherine hesitated, then tried to push it back into his hands. "It's not your day."

"That didn't stop me coming here."

"I haven't earned it."

"That," he said with barely concealed regret, "is my fault, not yours. Good night, Cat."

Stumbling onto the pavement a minute later, Micah staggered against the wall and tried to catch his breath.

That had been close.

CHAPTER TEN

October 19, 1812

THE BALLROOM WAS glittering, noisy, and Catherine was not supposed to be here.

Her gown was too tight. It had been a challenge, in truth, to tie it herself, corseted as she was in the latest fashion, but Catherine had managed it. Each of the red bows down the front were carefully created to hide the fact that this was a gown from yesteryear's fashion, but the red silk had not faded, and the ruffles at her sleeves were expertly mended.

Catherine took a deep breath.

The place was packed. Although a private ball—one which required an invitation to enter—Catherine had found it easy enough to slip in with a large crowd of what had to be cousins, for each had the same elegant air and refined manner.

But now she was alone, standing at the edge of the room, watching a line of dancers gracefully meander their way through the music.

"—delightful to see you, my dear—"

"—did not believe you could come, what a privilege to see you—"

"—hateful woman, why does she have to be here?"

Catherine allowed herself a small smile as she listened to the gossip weave around her.

There was nothing quite like a ball for transforming the way people spoke to each other. Friends outside could quite easily become enemies inside if the wrong step was made, the wrong person danced with, even a hint of scandal—

There he was. Catherine's stomach lurched as the sight of Micah de Petras appeared on the other side of the room, past the dancers, past a woman who was dressing down a footman for having spilled something…there he was.

Micah.

Her heart skipped a beat, like the fool she was. Was not he supposed to be the one looking across a crowded room and feeling faint at the sight of her?

Catherine sighed. It would be so much easier if she was not in love with him.

As her gaze followed him, she realized he was not alone. There was a woman on his arm. Before jealousy could find a home in her heart, the woman turned, and Catherine relaxed.

It was Sapphire. Sapphire de Petras.

Well, she was brave, Catherine thought darkly, *coming to a place like this, after what she suffered in Hyde Park.* But then, it could not have been the first time that she was affronted with such scandalous remarks, could it?

A little fury blazed in her stomach. *Some people were just…*

Catherine tried desperately to think of the words but was interrupted by a voice.

"My lady."

Catherine started and looked around to see a gentleman bowing to her. When he straightened up, she saw to her disappointment that it was Mr. Lister.

"Ah," she said helplessly.

"Miss Tetlow, I was devastated to miss our appointment," said Mr. Lister smoothly. "I must have mistaken the time, for though I waited there for near an hour, I was not gifted with the pleasure of your company."

Catherine's smile faltered. *Blast.* It was just her luck the dratted Mr. Lister would be the Penshaw ball, just when she had no use for him and every desire to avoid him.

It had not been possible all those nights ago to explain she had decided against taking him into her confidences and into her bed. After all, it was a delicate conversation at the best of times, and with Micah suddenly appearing and forcing Mr. Lister to leave—

"What a pity," she said aloud, seeing the odious man was waiting for her response. "But you will have to excuse me, Mr. Lister, I have just seen—"

She did not wait to finish her sentence. Striding away, just missing a pair of dancers who were joining the end of the line, Catherine breathed a sigh of relief at having escaped him. After putting out some gentle feelers, she had discovered the man was highly unpleasant and certainly not anyone she wished to associate with. Mrs. Goldsmith had been most specific.

"Miss de Petras," Catherine said.

Sapphire halted at the sound of her name, turning with delight. "Miss Tetlow!"

Catherine beamed. *Well, it was a success then.* She had managed to sneak into the ball, and at any point had expected to be asked to leave. She had already started to notice a few confused looks by those who could not place her face.

But now that Sapphire de Petras had acknowledged her, by name, all was well. No one would be so foolish as to think she did not belong here.

In truth, Catherine could already see a few people desperately trying to remember where they had seen her before, and she was in no doubt that within minutes, half the place would claim a close acquaintance with her.

"How lovely to see you," Catherine said, dropping a low curtsey.

The younger woman bobbed a curtsey in return. "Yes, I had hoped we would see each other again, after…well."

Catherine bit her lip. It was certainly not a pleasant situation to first meet.

Despite her better judgment, despite everything that told her she should certainly not do it, Catherine glanced at the gentleman beside Sapphire.

Micah was not looking at her.

Avidly not looking.

Something bold rose up in Catherine, and she said, "Good evening, Mr. de Petras."

Micah nodded, but he still did not look at her. A flicker of irritation seared her heart. How could he just stand there so close to her, knowing what they were to each other—or at least, what she hoped they would soon be to each other?

"Those are unusual earrings, Miss Tetlow," said Sapphire curiously. "Stone?"

Catherine smiled broadly. "Micah."

"Micah?"

That got his attention, as she knew it would. As Sapphire continued to examine the earrings, Micah's eyes flickered to hers.

Catherine's lips parted as she gasped. The intensity of that look, that connection which did not make any earthly sense, had shot through her like lightning.

Had he felt it, too? Was that why Micah did not seem able to remove his gaze?

"...quite unusual," Sapphire was saying. "How fascinating. Do not you think, Micah?"

"What?" Micah shook his head, then blinked at his sister. "You said something?"

Sapphire rolled her eyes, much to Catherine's amusement. "I do not know how your brother puts up with him, Miss Tetlow, he is constantly in a world of his own. I used to tease him it was his mistress that—oh, Lord, I probably should not have said that."

Now red splotches had appeared on Sapphire's face, and Catherine could not help but feel amused by the woman's lax tongue.

Certainly, she should not have said that!

"I am sorry, Miss de Petras, I was momentarily distracted by an intricate part of the dance, and did not hear a word you said," Catherine said smoothly with a knowing smile.

Would a wink at Micah be too much?

Probably—yet that did not stop Sapphire from glancing, expression still full of concern, at her brother, who winked.

Catherine gloried in the understanding they had. Surely Micah had never shared this with anyone else before?

"Now, Mr. de Petras," she said. "I think it high time you and I danced, don't you?"

That was enough to startle him from his silence.

"I beg your pardon?" said Micah.

Catherine permitted a flirtatious smile to curl her lips as a pair of gentlemen walked by, obviously appreciating her figure in a most lewd manner.

But that was all to the good, wasn't it? *Make sure Micah realized precisely what he was missing...*

"I said, we should dance," Catherine said. "We are at a ball, aren't we?"

"Yes, but—but you don't—you're not supposed to ask me to dance!"

There was real confusion in his tones, but Catherine could not help but notice a smile appear on Micah's face just as his eyes darkened with desire.

He wanted to. Oh, he wanted to do far more than dance with her, that was certain, but he could not do most of those things, at least, not here. Not without inviting scandal.

But he could dance with her...

Sapphire was looking between the two of them curiously, as though she had never seen two people flirt before. Perhaps she had not.

"I'm not supposed to ask you to dance?" repeated Catherine in a mystified voice as though she had never heard such a thing. "Why, then how did all those couples reach the set?"

Micah shook his head, his wry smile intact. Did he think her merely flirting? *Was this only a game to him?* "I'm supposed to ask you!"

And there it was. Her opening. "Well, go on then."

Micah's smile suddenly disappeared. "I did not mean—that isn't what I mean, Cat—Miss Tetlow, I—"

"I think in all honor, you are now bound," said Sapphire brightly. "Go on, Micah, I'll be waiting for you here when you are finished. Go and dance with the nice lady."

Shooting daggers at his sister and clearly desperate to avoid what was about to happen, Micah put out his hand with very poor grace.

"You were bold coming here tonight," Micah murmured as he walked her to the set as the music ended for this particular dance.

"I know."

"Was it worth it?"

"You tell me."

She curtseyed as she joined the ladies in the set and did not see Micah's expression as he turned to join the gentlemen—but she could guess.

He was furious. And intoxicated with her. Irritated beyond belief she was here. Desiring her beyond what was possible. It was everything she had hoped for, and now she had the pleasure of dancing with him, something they had never done before.

Considering everything they had shared in bed, it was rather strange to only now be sharing this social pleasantry.

The music began. Catherine stepped forward.

It was fortunate her mother had been most insistent that she learn all the dances of the day when a child, for otherwise, Catherine would have been at sea.

However, she turned to the right, curtseyed to the gentleman standing beside Micah—seeing with delight how irritated he was by this lack of her attention on himself—then offered her hands.

Micah took them with a fierce possessiveness.

"This feels…strange."

And just like that, her heart sank. Micah's words were whispered, intimate, it was true, but his statement was cold. Unfeeling. Distant.

She had to do something about it, had to draw him in. *Precisely how…*

"Why?" Catherine asked quietly as they parted to circle those beside them.

Micah did not speak again until they had joined each other in the dance, his voice low. "Because we are dancing together." All she had to do was raise an eyebrow, and he chuckled. "Well. We've never done this before."

Catherine smiled. "And yet you are actually quite good."

She stepped backward as the dance dictated, but not quickly enough to stop her from seeing the rush of desire on Micah's face. He wanted to be close to her, hated that the dance parted them.

And that was all to the good. If only he could see how being parted from her at all was not necessary, not if…

Catherine tried not to look at those watching the dancers. There were far too many people here, and as someone who was not formally invited, she knew almost no one else here.

But there were so many eyes on her—or was it, Micah?

"Everyone is staring," she murmured as they stepped together, hands intertwined, to promenade slowly down the set.

Micah chuckled. "That is because you are so beautiful."

"I think it more likely that they are astonished to see you stand up with anyone," countered Catherine, feeling her cheeks flush.

He snorted. "I've danced before."

"Not like this," Catherine breathed.

They were so close, her side pressed up against his as they slowly walked down the set, hand in hand, and it was like a wedding, like they were walking down an aisle toward a future that contained only each other.

Could he feel it? That wild sense they were traveling toward something wonderful?

"Besides," she added, hardly sure how she was able to speak but knowing she had to keep talking or she was likely to try to kiss him, "you are actually quite good. I suppose."

He chuckled, and Catherine beamed. Making Micah laugh was something so precious, so special. Who else could make him smile like that? Who else made her smile?

"You know, if I was not paying close attention," he murmured, his breath warm on Catherine's neck, making her shiver, "I would have thought we were…courting."

Catherine's breath caught in her throat. *Had he truly said that?*

Her heart skipped a beat, but she had to stay calm. Not only because she had to convince the man to fall in love with her—or admit he loved her, it amounted to the same thing—but because the dance was once again becoming more complex.

"Courting?" Catherine raised an eyebrow. "Aren't we?"

Micah rolled his eyes and muttered quietly, "One of us is certainly courting the other, I will admit that…but it is not me."

Was there a hint of reproach in his tone?

No, Catherine could not detect it. The way his eyes flashed with heat whenever they touched, the way his lips were parted…

Hungry.

"Yes, I suppose I am courting you," Catherine said with a laugh. *Well, there was no point in attempting to deny it, was there?* "Pursuing, I suppose, is more accurate a term."

"I'd call it pursuing."

"And how am I doing?"

Catherine took advantage of the movement of the dance and ensured she tilted her bodice just slightly, just enough so that Micah could see more of her breasts.

She heard him groan, watched him lick his lips, and felt a surge of triumph.

"I desire you, yes," Micah managed to say in a low voice, "but making me want you physically is not the same."

And the surge of triumph died away. "I know."

Catherine kept silent for almost a full minute as the dance came to its natural conclusion. What else could she say? He was right, of course, though she would not give him the satisfaction of hearing it from her lips.

Seducing Micah was not the challenge. She performed that duty every week, though it had ceased to be a duty and had become a celebration long ago. But if she could do no more than that…why, she would be nothing else but a mistress, wouldn't she?

The dance ended. Catherine curtseyed, trying to remain balanced as her legs shook beneath her. It was intoxicating to be sure, dancing with Micah, but she had done that now and seemed no further in her quest to make him fall in love with her.

She was running out of options, of opportunities, of—

Catherine gasped. Her hand had been taken by Micah, and it was not the delicate perfunctory touch of a gentleman after a dance.

No, this was determined. Eager.

He did not have to say a word. She could feel the desire in his fingertips, knew what he wanted, what he craved, and the same desire had been building in her the moment she had first seen him.

With Micah leading, they wended their way through the crowd, entirely ignoring his sister who seemed happily engaged in conversation with a gentleman Catherine vaguely recognized, and within moments, they were in a small silent room.

"Cat—"

Catherine pulled Micah toward her and kissed him hard on the mouth. Oh, it was heavenly.

She moaned, unable to help herself. Micah knew just what she liked, knew just how she wanted to be kissed and—

"Micah," Catherine panted, breaking the kiss.

He looked at her with lust-hazed eyes. "Cat?"

She swallowed, trying to regain control. Kissing Micah, it was as though the world was right and nothing could stop her happiness. But she could not let this continue. Not without assurances that right now, Micah was not willing to give her.

"It's not Thursday."

Micah groaned, lowering his head to kiss her neck. "I don't care. I want you."

Catherine's eyes closed, unable to bear the passion pouring down onto her. How easy it would be to just let this happen, to allow him to take her here in this parlor, but—

"No," she said firmly, and Micah raised his head at the intensity of her words. "No, on Thursdays you own me, you buy me. But not today. Today, if you want me, it must be for...f-for something else."

He blinked. "Something else?"

Catherine knew she had gone too far, pushed him beyond endurance. "Yes."

Micah examined her, blinking as his gaze became clearer. "You are in earnest."

"I told you I would make you fall in love with me," Catherine breathed, looking up into the eyes of the gentleman she adored. "And I meant it."

"But just this once—"

"There is no just this once on any other day but Thursday," she interjected, his hands still on her waist, hands she wished would never be removed. "I need more."

"More?"

Catherine nodded.

For a moment, Micah just stood, hesitant, clearly unable to either understand her or obey her. Then a smile crept across his face, one she had never seen before. *Was it...shy?*

"I'll give you what I can, Cat," he said quietly. "I...I have never felt as safe with any other woman. Never felt so attracted to them—"

"Micah—"

"Body and soul," he interrupted, as though guessing her complaint. "You are kind, Cat, and considerate, and when I am with you…"

Catherine's breath caught in her throat. She had never heard him so earnest, never heard him so…vulnerable.

"I am not in love with you," came Micah's quiet voice. "But what I feel for you is certainly more than a man should feel for his mistress. I care for you. I want you, and not just because you satisfy my desire. Because you satisfy something…something deeper."

She would take it. Catherine lifted her face to be kissed, moaned as he pressed his mouth to hers in a reverent, loving way, not merely the hot-headed eagerness of a man needing to be bedded.

She would take it. *For now.*

Chapter Eleven

October 20, 1812

WHEN MICAH AWOKE, it was to discover to his great surprise that although he had managed to find his way home—an impressive feat after one of Penshaw's balls—he had not managed to make it home alone.

He groaned softly as he turned in bed to see a blonde sprawled beside him.

Well, this was going to be awkward. Either she was a lady of the night, in which case he owed her money he did not have, or she was a lady of Society in which case there was going to be a rather strained conversation about matrimony, and how he wanted none of it.

Only when she stirred did Micah suddenly realize.

It wasn't a lady of the night or the *ton*. It was Catherine.

Micah blinked, then looked more closely around the place. He hadn't made his way home, after all, it seemed. He had managed to get back to Catherine's lodgings.

A slow smile crept across his face. Well, he could not have imagined a better outcome to his dilemma. He had nothing to fear from her in the way of marriage proposals or attempts to extort him for money. He gave her enough as it was.

He slowly stroked her bare back with his finger.

Catherine stirred, a smile on her face, and slowly opened her eyes. Her smile widened. "Good morning."

A strange sort of joy, unfamiliar to him before and flooding his body, radiated through Micah. "Good morning."

He leaned forward and kissed her before wondering what on earth had possessed him to do so. It was not as though he had any deep affection for her, yet the action felt natural.

Catherine sighed happily, then suddenly her eyes started open. "You're here."

"I hope that is not too much of a bother," teased Micah. "I know you have a hectic social life, but—"

"No, I mean...I mean you're *here*," she repeated as though that clarified the matter.

Micah stared, waiting for further explanation, but it appeared none was coming.

And why should there be? He was remarkably comfortable here, Catherine's bed was always far superior to his own anyway, and it was delightful to have a view of her naked form this early in the morning.

What a way to wake up. Why, any gentleman would be fortunate—

Just in time, Micah caught himself from thinking something he certainly should not be. Not if he wanted to remain a bachelor. And he did. No gamble by a wench as beautiful as Catherine was going to catch him.

"You're here," she repeated, a half-smile on her lips. "You're always gone by the time I wake up. You slip away in the night, and I wake up alone."

Micah swallowed. Now that she had pointed that out, it was difficult to deny. She was right; Micah had a habit, a rule even, of never being here when Catherine awoke. It was far too akin to being something to each other they were not.

"I know I'm usually gone, but I thought I'd stay," he found himself saying. "Just for a while. If that is not injurious to your plans?"

Catherine chuckled sleepily, her eyelids starting to drift shut again. "Injurious to my plans? What do you think I do all day, make calls? Welcome duchesses and countesses to my table, leave gilded cards on marble mantelpieces?"

She laughed, but Micah swallowed. *What did she do all day?*

It was certainly not something he had ever considered. Cat was…Cat. She was Thursdays. She was what he looked forward to all week, enjoyed in a hedonistic play of pleasure, and then left, early, before the sun was up.

What Catherine did when he was not here was something he had not considered, and even now it was impossible for him to guess what it was. She must do something, he supposed.

"Well," Micah said rather awkwardly. "I thought I would stay. For a bit."

Catherine opened her eyes and raised an eyebrow. "My goodness, Micah de Petras. Are you starting to care for me? Just a little?"

"Not a whit," he lied swiftly with an answering smile.

It was his heart that was betraying him. Micah could have said the words quite easily without any hesitation, and indeed he had done before.

But that did not make the words any more true.

They *were* false. His heart skipped a beat as Catherine turned, lying on her back and smiling up at him. There was such trust there, such honesty, and it was…attractive.

Micah had given very little thought to what attracted him to a woman. Beyond the obvious. He had bedded tall women, short women, women with curves that he sank into, and women so lithe he had to pin them down on the bed as he worshipped them.

A woman's beauty came in many forms.

But a woman's character…that had been so wholly separate from his idea of beauty that Micah had not considered how the two were connected.

He could see it now. There was something about Catherine, something radiating beauty far deeper than her skin.

"You're staring at me."

"That's not a crime, is it?" Micah said with a laugh.

He pushed the feelings, whatever they were, down hard, past his heart, deeper and deeper until he could barely feel them anymore.

He did not have to be tied to his emotions, that's what women were, weren't they? Utterly captivated by their hearts. Well, he had no such intention. He had made a gamble, and he was not going to lose.

"Breakfast," said Micah decidedly.

Catherine frowned. "Breakfast? Micah, you cannot possibly think I will be cooking for you. Have you seen a kitchen in this place?"

Micah opened his mouth, then closed it again. Well, he had rather assumed the situation at Parson's Buildings was like his own. A kitchen below that all the bachelors who had taken lodgings in the residence could call down to and order tea, hot crumpets, kippers, or toast in the mornings.

And that was just breakfast.

But evidently, if the look on Catherine's face was anything to go by...

"Oh," he said helplessly. "Then..."

She giggled, and all the tension in the room disappeared. "You dolt! I have bread and butter, I'll do us toast over the fire."

Without another word, Catherine crept out of the bed, and Micah's breath hitched in his throat.

For all his thoughts of beauty, there was something very primal in the way he appreciated Catherine's body. *Dear God, to think that every week he—*

"You are looking at me."

"I see no reason to deny it," said Micah wryly as he leaned back and watched Catherine pull a gown on.

It wasn't the brilliant red silk gown she had worn yesterday at the ball, it was calmer, plainer, yet still very Catherine. A delicate apricot pink, with elegant piping of cream down the bodice and sleeves.

Micah swallowed. *She was very beautiful.*

"Will you help me?"

He blinked. "Help you?"

Catherine was smiling but had turned away, holding out the two ribbons at the back of her gown. "I usually make do on my own, but as you are here…"

Her voice trailed away as she waited for him.

Micah's stomach lurched, and it had nothing to do with the very sudden movement he made, leaping out of bed toward her. *Any excuse to be close to her*, he told himself. He was doing her this favor only because it benefited him.

And dear God, did it benefit him. He could feel her warmth, even through the gown, could feel his own desire growing as he stood there, utterly naked, carefully tying the woman into a piece of clothing that was hiding the very best of her.

"Micah?"

He tried not to groan, and instead satisfied himself by gently kissing the side of her neck. "Cat."

She did not push him away, did not encourage him, but lightly tilted her neck. "You are supposed to be doing up my gown."

"I'm far more inclined to undo it," Micah murmured, kissing her again.

She shivered under his touch—but then she stepped away.

"If you cannot do it—"

"Fine, fine, I'll tie you in," said Micah hurriedly.

To lose a chance to be close to her…

"There," he said, just a hint of sadness in his tone. "And I suppose you want me to get dressed now, too, do you?"

Catherine turned and looked appreciatively—and rather obviously—up and down his naked form. "Did I say that?"

It was all Micah could do not to pull Catherine into his arms, push her down onto the bed, push up her skirts, and ravage her until she cried out his name…but his stomach gurgled.

"I get the message," she laughed, stepping to the door.

"Come through when you're dressed."

Micah sighed heavily. This was not the usual way of things with them at all, and he was discovering rather to his mingled delight and horror that he was enjoying himself.

Enjoying a morning of banter, quips, kisses, and breakfast—with a mistress?

He must be out of his mind…

By the time Micah had dressed—at least, pulled on breeches, boots, and thrown on his shirt—there was the delicious smell of toast wafting under the door. Catherine had evidently got the fire going.

When he stepped into what he thought of as her parlor, Catherine was perched on the end of a sofa by the fire, with a toasting fork in her hands. On the end of it were two pieces of bread slowly becoming toast.

"Butter?" asked Catherine lightly. "I have marmalade, too, if you want it."

"I'm a jam man, myself," Micah said, dropping onto the sofa and placing his arms around her.

She put up no fight but merely smiled, and for a moment, Micah forgot himself.

Then he rose swiftly. He was not going to slip into this domestic scene, he was not! This was Catherine's attempt to gain his affection, and he would not be so easily manipulated.

"Tea?"

Micah smiled, despite himself. "Yes please."

The kettle hung over the fire at the other end, and Catherine expertly placed the toasting fork just close enough to the flames to continue toasting the bread as she lifted the kettle off its hook. Two cups were waiting.

"You were expecting me."

Catherine raised an eyebrow. "I had just come from my bed-cham—my boudoir, Micah. I knew precisely that you were here."

Ah. Of course, that should have been obvious.

Shaking his head, forcing from it any foolish thoughts of

conspiracy and planning, Micah sat instead on the armchair opposite where Catherine had been perched.

Within a few minutes—minutes they spent in companionable silence—Catherine passed him a plate with two slices of toast, enough butter to sink a ship, and the jar of marmalade.

"I have no jam, I'm afraid. Tea's on the side for you there," she said lightly. "Now tell me. You have lodgings in London, yet your family lives here, too. I know you don't...well."

"See eye to eye on all things," Micah supplied with a dry laugh.

This toast really was excellent. When was the last time he'd had toast directly from the toasting fork to his plate? There was something very homely and delicious about toast you had burnt yourself.

Catherine nodded as she placed two more pieces of bread on the toasting fork. "Yes, precisely. But I cannot imagine many gentlemen take that step, even with family that is a little...differently opinionated. Why?"

It was an interesting question, and one that Micah would pay complete attention to, once he had got this last dollop of marmalade to behave.

"Micah!"

"What?" Micah said hurriedly, looking up to see Catherine had already finished toasting her bread and was now waiting for the marmalade. *Good God, how long had he been spreading it?* "Oh, here you go."

Their fingers grazed, just ever so slightly, as he passed her the sticky jar. Micah expected it this time, though he was still none the wiser from where it came from.

A spark, a frisson, there was no other word for it.

And then it was gone.

Or was it gone? Micah could feel something odd in his chest ...

It was most unaccountable.

"Micah?"

"Yes? Yes," he said hurriedly, taking a bite of the toast and marmalade and moaning with delight. "This really is very good."

"Seville orange and brandy. Tell me why you took your own lodgings."

Micah hesitated for a moment, focusing instead on the delicious breakfast, but he could not avoid answering forever. "You don't know my family."

He had intended to say something far more impressive. Something that explained the way he felt, justified the action he had taken years ago to escape his family—as much as one could escape the de Petras family while still living in London.

But apparently, his words had not captured those feelings.

Catherine sipped her tea. "I did not think they were that bad."

A sting of irritation rose in Micah's chest. "I did not say they were bad, I just—"

"I have heard you speak much about them, and other than a desire to see you more than once a week, which I share," said Catherine delicately, "and a propensity to hound you about getting married, I have heard no ill of them."

Micah's jaw tightened, but then, he could not argue with her.

When she put it like that, his family seemed normal. It was not as though they had done something ridiculous like ask Miss Ashbrooke, noted matchmaker, to find him a bride.

But still, it was frustrating, and that frustration had forced him from his home.

Only then did Micah realize that he still considered his childhood home...home.

"It's not that they are bad people—most of them are very good people, really," said Micah helplessly, taking another bite of toast as if that would save him from having to explain himself. Catherine waited patiently, and he swallowed his mouthful. "I just...I am not head of the family."

There. It was said. It still sounded petulant, saying it aloud, but Micah was certain he had given Catherine sufficient justification to understand his reasoning now.

Yet apparently not. "Well, of course not," she said, nose

scrunching in confusion. "Your father is still alive, that would be most indecorous, Micah."

Micah sighed. "Not my father…my mother."

"Your mother?"

He heard the surprise in her voice before he lifted his head and saw her expression, but it was one he knew well.

Everyone was surprised to hear it was Opal de Petras, not Jasper, who was the head of the family. Some people thought it a jest, a trick—until they saw the two of them in public.

"It's a tradition from my mother's side, obviously," Micah tried to explain, finding the same old phrasing trotted out of his lips that he had used at Cambridge. *Again, and again, he'd had to explain…* "She's Italian, and her people—it's the woman who inherits, you see? My father's shipping business keeps the family, he's done remarkably well and continues to grow the thing, but it's my mother's fortune Coral will inherit when she takes up the mantle."

"Coral?" Catherine was staring, agog.

"Coral."

Understanding appeared finally to be dawning on her face. "You are not the heir."

"The only gentleman in London unable to keep his own house, plan his own future, inherit his own wealth," said Micah, trying as best he could to keep the bitterness out, and failing miserably. "So, you see, it's a point of contention between us, Coral and me. Oh, I would never dream of attempting open rebellion," he added with a laugh. "My mother would never allow it, and though I may not always get on with Coral, I love her. Sometimes I even like her. She is my sister."

"Sisters are important," came Catherine's quiet reply.

Micah shook his head with a laugh. "What would you know of sisters?"

"Well, I have one," said Catherine lightly, meeting his gaze. "Does that make me an expert?"

His mouth fell open. *Sister?* Catherine didn't have a sister, did she—she had no siblings. No parents, no siblings, no family of any sort. Why else would she...

It was a rather unpleasant thought, but Micah forced himself to follow it to the end. Why else would she permit herself to be a mistress of a gentleman with no fortune and little ability to protect her, should her reputation be quashed?

"You...you don't have a sister," he said rather foolishly.

Catherine sipped her tea, then placed the cup and saucer down. "And how do you know that?"

"B-Because," stammered Micah, "because you've never mentioned her!"

"I have a brother, too, and he certainly exists, even though I have never spoken of him to you," Catherine said quietly. "I support them."

Support them?

She laughed, and the tension in the room disappeared. "Goodness, you should see your face, Micah—you think you know me? You think because you bed me, you have seen all of me?"

Micah swallowed. *Now she said it, it seemed obvious.* But Catherine Tetlow, a sister! A sister with two siblings who she supports?

Wait a moment. *Supports?*

"How old are these siblings?" he asked curiously.

"Thirteen and twelve," she replied archly. "And they are not my secret illegitimate children if that is what you are truly asking."

Heat seared Micah's cheeks. "I wasn't—"

"When our parents died, there was nothing left after my father's gambling debts," Catherine said. "I found a woman to take them in, care for them in exchange for pay, and I..."

Her voice trailed away but it was evident to what she was referring.

To him. She meant him.

Micah's stomach curled in on itself. He had always considered his meetings with Catherine to be about pleasure; hers as well as his. He had always ensured she left their couplings just as satisfied as he was, thinking only of that moment. The money was an afterthought, one that worked well for him. It prevented any romantic entanglements, any emotions he would not be able to return.

But all this time, to Catherine, it was…about money?

Then he caught her eye and saw the tiredness, the defiant pride, the determination.

And his heart softened. "You have done well to care for them all this time."

"Bearing such a burden alone is not one I would have chosen for myself, "she admitted, finishing the last of her toast. "But in five or six years or so—"

"Five or six years?"

"John will have a decision to make. University or an apprenticeship."

Micah stared. "He…he is at school then?"

There it was, another flicker of pain. "Not—not exactly. I am sure, once my circumstances turn around—"

"When you win that one hundred pounds from me, for falling in love with you?" Micah said with a mischievous smile.

The smile that met his was no less mischievous. "Exactly. It will be easier then."

And he could see it, the weight of responsibility, the burden on her shoulders, the worry that filled her eyes when she thought no one was looking. How could he have missed it? How had he not seen the weight she carried?

"I…I did not know."

"You never asked," said Catherine. "Where do you think all your ten pounds go? I hardly live in the lap of luxury."

An elegant hand raised to gesture at the room they were sitting in, but Micah did not look round. He was too busy looking at the woman before him. A proud, independent, clearly determined, beautiful woman.

One he had underestimated.

CHAPTER TWELVE

October 27, 1812

"I JUST DO not know why you bother," came the heavy sigh from behind her.

Catherine smiled at the small looking glass she had managed to balance on the shelf where she kept her meager collection of books. "I know you don't."

"You are beautiful!"

"I know you think that, Mrs. Goldsmith, but still," said Catherine lightly as she attempted to weave another golden thread into her blonde curls. "I like to make the effort."

For whom, she was not going to say. At least, not out loud. It was not ladylike to admit to pursuing a gentleman, after all, and the more she tried not to think about just how much she wanted this evening to go well, the more her heart fluttered.

Traitorous thing.

Still, the preparations had gone well so far. Mrs. Goldsmith had been an absolute dream, boiling kettles of water on her own fire to add to her own. She would never have got the bath full of hot water without her—at least, not today, at any rate.

The bath itself had been wonderful; Catherine could not recall the last time she'd had a bath, a hot one.

The delicate rose soap she had been keeping for a special

occasion had been taken out of its box and finally lathered. And what a treat it was—no wonder she had kept it for three years, waiting, waiting for the right occasion to use it.

Catherine smiled as she raised another hand to wend a golden thread through her hair. Why, with every movement she made, she could smell the delicate fragrance on her skin.

If that was not enough to impress Micah—

"Another one?" Mrs. Goldsmith tutted as Catherine finished tying the thread just below her nape. "I do not believe I have ever seen you so careful of your attire, girl."

Catherine let the comment go. She had been neighbors with Mrs. Goldsmith for the best part of a year, after all. Eventually, some of the formalities were going to have to slide.

"Well, this is a very important night," she said aloud.

"Important night? Important night? Unless it was your own wedding night, I do not think I have seen a woman put this much effort to please just one man," said Mrs. Goldsmith with a sniff. As Catherine turned around, she leered. "Unless you are thinking of entertaining more than one—"

"Mrs. Goldsmith!"

"I'm just saying, is all," shrugged the older woman with a wicked grin, "I may not be in the flush of my youth anymore, but I have memories."

Scandalized by the suggestion—and what it revealed of her neighbor—Catherine turned back to the looking glass.

There was little more that she could do for her appearance now. Her hair was carefully coiffed and pinned into place, the golden threads lighting up her face almost like a halo in this candlelight.

She had attempted to prize enough of the lip rouge from the packet but there was precious little left. Only after Catherine had wet her finger and tried to spread the color around was she happy.

Her gown, a red silk one that flowed gracefully down her bodice to the floor was of the latest style. Mrs. Goldsmith said she could borrow it, and with only a little adjustment, it fitted.

Catherine pursed her lips. *If she did not secure Micah's heart soon, she would be forced to purchase a new gown.*

"What's his name, again?"

She turned to see Mrs. Goldsmith had helped herself to a seat—which, after all the help she had given her that afternoon, she was more than entitled to. In fact, Catherine felt ashamed she had not offered.

"Micah," she said shyly.

It felt strange, Micah's name on her tongue before someone else. But then, London was a large place, there was no reason that Mrs. Goldsmith would know—

"That de Petras boy?" Mrs. Goldsmith's face lit up. "A handsome chap, I would say, from what I've seen of him. Comes here regular, don't he?"

Catherine met her neighbor's eye. They had never discussed just how Catherine was able to afford her rooms in Parson's Buildings; it was a conversation only to be had with those she was intimately acquainted with.

"I...uh..." She should have had a plan, a sentence she could trot out to explain precisely who she was and what she did to survive.

But there was no judgment in her neighbor's eyes, just sadness. "We all took to it at one point or another, my girl. There's no shame in it."

Catherine swallowed. "I challenged him to a wager."

"Oh?"

"That he would fall in love with me."

Mrs. Goldsmith snorted with laughter. "You bet that he— he..."

Her voice trailed away as she took in Catherine's determined air. "He will fall in love with me."

"Aye. I don't doubt that," came the gentle reply. "Well then, I see why you're putting so much time into your clothing and face and the like. But is he worth it, my dear? Falling in love does not account for everything, especially these days."

There had never been a Mr. Goldsmith, Catherine recalled—at least, not one who was ever introduced to her, and one had never been mentioned.

She focused intently on not checking her neighbor's hand for a ring. "You don't know Micah like I do. He's...he is worthy of striving for."

Catherine flushed as she spoke. It was odd, speaking of Micah aloud like this. Most of the time, she was content to think about him alone. She had once mentioned him to John and Mary, but they had asked so many questions about 'Catty's friend Micah' that she had never mentioned him again.

"You're right," said Mrs. Goldsmith with a grin. "I don't know him. Tell me about him—describe him for me, and I shall tell you whether he is worth the effort."

Catherine had to smile. *Oh, if only it was so easy.* Did Mrs. Goldsmith think she'd had any choice?

"He..."

Words failed her as she sat gently down on the end of the sofa. How did one describe Micah? How could all of his inconsistencies, complexities, and downright idiocy be captured in just a few words?

"He..." Catherine swallowed, fingers tangling in her lap. "He's kind. Handsome of course, but kind. That was what drew me to him at the very beginning, his kindness. The way he looks at the world, it's as though he's hoping for the best even if he knows the world might disappoint him."

Mrs. Goldsmith raised an eyebrow. "Is that so?"

"Headstrong and very foolish," Catherine continued with a laugh, her gaze drifting in the distance, seeing something not in her rooms. "Always determined to be right and rarely managing it, but...but there's a cleverness in him. A wit I have never found in any other man."

"Or woman, I'll be bound."

"No one is like him, no one I have ever met. His boldness

goes beyond decorum, and yet he has never made me feel in the way or…or anything like that." Catherine swallowed. "He has only made me feel safe and adored."

Her words hung in the air, almost shimmering, visible with the passion she spoke.

She should not have been so open. Catherine regretted it instantly, knew she should not have been so courageous as to speak about a gentleman like that, but—

"Well worth the catch then," Mrs. Goldsmith said quietly.

Catherine shifted her gaze and met the wry smile of her neighbor. "If I can catch him."

"Oh, I have no doubt of that," said the older woman easily. "He's not blind, is he?"

"No, but he's seen me…all of me, you understand, for the last two years," admitted Catherine. "If he was so easily caught, he would have been mine for a while. I've…I've done all I can, and he still doesn't want me."

It was painful to admit, but Catherine could not lie to herself any longer. She was not a lady of Society, who could dazzle him with jewels, talks of her country estate, or rides in the forest.

No, she had nothing but charm and good looks to recommend her, and she had barely made a difference with those, as far as she could see.

"He doesn't want me," said Catherine, trying to force brightness into her voice but failing miserably as she rose to turn to the looking glass. "I'm being foolish, I think, even attempting this tonight. If I was wise—"

"If you were wise, you'd be out of here sooner rather than later, give yourself more time tonight," came the response from behind her.

Catherine whirled around to see Mrs. Goldsmith rising slowly. "I beg your pardon?"

"All I says is, it doesn't sound as though you're not able to catch him," said Mrs. Goldsmith simply. "Sounds to me as though he doesn't trust himself to be caught. He don't trust himself to fall in love."

And with that, she left.

Catherine stood, half in shock, half in delight at her neighbor's words. *Doesn't trust himself to fall in love?*

Could it be that simple? Could she unlock Micah's heart somehow, demonstrate to him that it was not only wonderful to fall in love, but that the affection was already returned?

That in fact, if he was willing to give himself to her, she was already waiting with her heart, ready to hand it over to him?

It was a heady thought, and one that completely consumed Catherine as she made the last adjustments to her apparel—ensuring to pop the earrings Micah had gifted her through her ears—and when she arrived outside Micah's lodgings, Catherine's heart had twisted itself inside out and round and round more times than she could count.

That had to account for why her breath was short, why her hands tingled as they pulled her pelisse closer to her.

What she was doing…well, it was rather rebellious, wasn't it?

It was not Thursday, not a day they had promised to each other—more, she was merely turning up outside his lodgings.

Micah had never forbidden her to do such a thing, but he had clearly never considered a need to. Their arrangement was in her rooms, and that was where they had always met.

Save for that encounter at his family's home, of course.

Catherine shivered, but the night was warm. It had been a level of intimacy she had not expected, and now she was demanding even more of him.

He would never expect it.

"Catherine?" Micah said blankly.

Catherine attempted her most seductive smile as the door opened, but she could tell it was not entirely working. For a start, Micah seemed utterly confused to find her standing on the landing outside his lodging. It had been rather difficult to persuade the man below to let her in, but now she was here…

Well, wasn't he supposed to look pleased?

"You…you look incredible," Micah breathed.

And in that instant, her confidence returned. Catherine smiled, shrugging as though this was how she looked every single minute of every single day. "This old thing?"

She plucked the silk gown, being careful not to tear it. Mrs. Goldsmith would not thank her for that.

Micah swallowed, and Catherine delighted in the way his Adam's apple bobbed. "You…you smell of roses. Damn, Cat. Is—is that gold in your hair?"

And all the hours of preparation, all the worry about getting it right faded away. Catherine stood, triumphant in the certainty that everything she had done to impress was landing precisely the way she wanted.

"I suppose beautiful young ladies do not receive an invitation across your threshold?" she said archly.

Micah blinked, as though collecting himself. "Thresh—yes, yes, come in. My word."

He stepped aside, and Catherine walked into his lodgings.

She had not known what to expect. Micah was not a wealthy gentleman, not compared to many who strutted on London's streets, but he was wealthy enough to support her and at least three other mistresses at one point, she knew, so he was certainly not a man in need of additional funds.

That was clear in the state of his lodgings. A man in some sort of livery was evidently a servant, and was just tidying away what appeared to be a large dinner from a mahogany table in one corner. A sofa and several armchairs sat around a fire on the other side of the room.

Catherine's stomach rumbled. She was not going to think about the last time she'd had a hot meal.

"I—well, I did not expect you," said Micah, hurrying to move a few things. "That will be all, Holland."

The man bowed. "Very good, sir."

They were alone in a moment, Micah standing awkwardly in the center of the room.

Catherine walked around slowly, taking it all in, giving herself time to think. Well, she had been invited in, and there had always been a chance he would have refused such a request.

"It is lovely to see you, Cat—"

"Thank you," she said sweetly.

"But I...well, damnit all, I don't think I have it in me to bed you this evening."

Catherine blinked. Micah was smiling awkwardly, and there was a rather tired look around his eyes.

Didn't have it in him to bed her?

"I've spent most of the day with Coral and her husband and that baby of theirs," confessed Micah with a wry laugh. "And my mother. I'm done in. I...well, I would rather have good company."

Catherine swallowed. Startled was not quite the right expression—she had never known Micah to be unwilling to take her to bed and touch her until she cried out his name.

But then, their meetings were always on his terms, were they not? Always dictated by the day of the week, always designed for a bedding.

This, then, was an opportunity to meet him on an entirely different setting. An opportunity, in fact, to show him what she was like when not naked and writhing under him...

"Perfect," she said with a smile. "In that case, let's have some fun instead."

Micah groaned. "I told you, I have not the strength to—"

"Oh, you and your one-track mind," Catherine chided him as she rolled her eyes and removed her pelisse, throwing it onto an armchair. "There's more than one way to have fun, you know. Where's your pack of cards?"

Micah blinked. "Pack of—"

"Cards, Micah, cards," she repeated, sitting down cross legged on the floor by the fire. "I know you must have one, and all I ask is that it's not your marked deck."

"I don't have a—"

"Don't you?" Catherine raised her eyebrows.

Micah was gracious enough to look a little bashful. "I'll go and find it—wine?"

"Always," she said sweetly.

When Micah returned with a pack of cards, Catherine was ready and waiting with a new plan. Show him what it was to adore her, yes, but not just her body, her company.

"Now, do you know piquet?" she asked, indicating he should be seated.

Micah hesitated. "Sitting on the floor?"

Catherine smiled, pouring her winning charm into the expression. "If it's good enough for me…"

After twenty minutes of careful explanations, four demonstrations, and a practice round, Micah still appeared to have absolutely no idea what to do.

"I'll never get the hang of this," he said with a laugh. "How do you do it?"

"Win, every time?" Catherine giggled, shifting her legs under her skirts to better balance as she pulled together all the cards. "'Tis just my winning nature, I suppose."

Micah snorted as he finished his glass of wine. "No, it must be more than that—I have never lost so badly in my life! You are cheating!"

"It's your pack of cards."

"That accounts for almost nothing," said Micah with a laugh. "You know this game inside and out—I would not be surprised if you had invented it just to torture me!"

Catherine laughed. "Just because you are losing!"

Their laughter mingled, the air warm and the atmosphere light, and Catherine could have sung.

This was what she wanted. Well, one of the many things she wanted, bedding Micah, laughing with Micah, playing cards with Micah, dancing with Micah…

As long as she had him, that was all she wanted. All she needed. The trouble was ensuring the sensation was reciprocated.

As she carefully dealt the cards—ensuring kings were right at the bottom of the pack—Catherine smiled at the handsome gentleman whose cheeks were flushed and eyes were bright.

"Do you wish to make this more interesting?"

Micah groaned. "I'm already losing, and you want to make it more complicated?"

"I said more interesting, not complicated," corrected Catherine, heart singing as she dealt out the next hand. "We could add money to the outcome."

"Another wager?"

"I will make you fall in love with me."

Catherine swallowed. Sometimes she forgot she had made that silly wager. In a strange way, it had been foolish of her to give Micah a warning of what she was attempting.

Making him fall in love with her was indeed far harder than she had expected, but that should have been anticipated, now he knew her intentions.

Still, nothing ventured... "Another wager."

Micah laughed, shaking his head. "Absolutely not! Besides, aren't you already losing our first one?"

Catherine swallowed, her gaze catching his as Micah's laughter died away. "Am I?"

The moment between them was heavy with meaning, meaning unspoken by them both. Catherine's breath caught in her throat, her lungs tight, and anticipation of something great billowed in her stomach.

At any moment, he was about to say—

"M-My turn to start," Micah said, dropping his gaze to the cards.

Catherine remembered to breathe. "Yes. Yes, your turn."

It was not to be; at least, she tried to console herself as they played cards into the night, laughter and wine flowing, it was not to be tonight.

But she still managed a small victory, even if it was not the one she had entered Micah's rooms for. By the time the dawn arrived, she was still in his lodgings. More, she was in his bed.

And in a strike toward her goal, he had indeed not bedded her…but that had not stopped Micah reaching for Catherine in the night, pulling her close into his embrace, and kissing her gently just below the ear.

CHAPTER THIRTEEN

November 1, 1812

T HE LAST TIME Micah had paced this continuously, it was just before he was about to inform his parents that he had taken lodgings in town—without their consent.

With their money, but without their consent.

Micah dragged a hand through his hair as he reached the end of the corridor and turned around again to pace back to the other side. His heart thumped painfully, and there was a strange sort of tension in his shoulders that he did not appreciate but could not shake.

This was madness. This was foolishness, to the extreme.

And yet he was considering it.

"Besides, aren't you already losing our first one?"

A foolish smile came over him as he halted again, just outside the door that he could not bring himself to go through, but knew he must.

He must go in there and talk to her. Catherine. *Tell her…*

Micah swallowed, his mouth suddenly dry. *Tell her what?* Tell her that he was starting to…to wonder whether…

"I will make you fall in love with me."

Dragging a hand through his hair once more and returning to his pacing, Micah tried desperately to convince himself his emotions, much less his heart, were not involved at all.

He had never fallen in love, never had to even think about it. Why, he'd balanced four mistresses at once before, and never accidentally caught feelings for any of them.

But none of them were Catherine Tetlow.

"Besides, aren't you already losing our first one?"

It had been that evening which had done it. Micah had awoken, Catherine nestled into him, and he had felt…wonderful. As though all was right with the world. As though nothing else could change, for he wanted things to stay precisely the way they were. Fighting it ever since had made no difference. One could not fight what had already settled in one's heart.

Micah shivered, attempting to convince himself it was due to the cold and not his frantic thoughts. The door along from Catherine's was opening, and Micah drew himself up, as tall as he could. It was not as though he had to explain himself here. He had every right to be here, every—

"Good evening," said the woman as she closed her door. "Micah de Petras, I presume."

Micah stared. *Now, this was something new.* He had never before considered he had a reputation so dire, he could be recognized on sight by any woman who came across him!

"I-I…" he stammered.

The woman smiled. She was older than him, perhaps closer to his parents' age, but there was a twinkle in her eyes that told him she had not forgotten the pleasures of this world.

"Yes, I thought so," said the woman with an acid smile as she began to descend the stairs. "Give my best wishes to young Miss Catherine, won't you?"

Micah stared after the woman, and only when the sound of the door to the street opened and shut did he realize he had not actually replied to her.

Blast. How on earth did she…

He swallowed, turning his gaze to Catherine's door. She was far more wily than he had ever given her credit for. Perhaps that was why he...

Well, there was nothing he could do about it standing out here, Micah thought sternly. He needed to go in there and do something. Say something, perhaps, if he was foolish to permit his mind to entirely overtake him.

Which, when in Catherine's company, was possible...

Micah cringed at the sound of his knock on Catherine's door. It felt so—so cheap. Catherine was no cheap courtesan, no lady of the night, who could be picked up for a few shillings. He should have a bell installed here—how, precisely, he was not sure, but—

"Micah."

He blinked. The door had opened, and there stood before him a vision in red silk. It was Catherine. She was wearing the same gown she had worn for the Penshaw ball, or at least one so similar to it that they were indistinguishable, and she was wearing his earrings again.

Micah's stomach lurched. Why did he feel such a sense of pride, of possessiveness when he saw Catherine wearing a gift of his? And why had he not gifted her with jewels before?

But there was more. Long cream gloves covered her hands, pulled up to her elbows, and—was that some sort of tiara in her hair?

"Micah," Catherine repeated, waving a hand before his eyes. "Micah? Are you well?"

Micah cleared his throat and stepped forward, deciding not to answer aloud as he forced Catherine to take a step back.

"Micah, you cannot just—"

"You look...nice."

She looked nice? Micah groaned inwardly and turned to face her as Catherine shut the door. Could he not think of a more potent thing to say? Anything would have been better than that— a statement about the weather would have sufficed!

Or rather, it would not have. For a comment about the unseasonable warmth they were experiencing would in no way go to explain just what he was doing here, on a Sunday, completely out of their agreed schedule.

Once he could explain it to himself, perhaps then he could explain it to her…

The fire was dampened down in the grate, and there was a general aura of untidiness in what Micah still considered Catherine's parlor.

"You are going out?"

It was a foolish question, Micah knew that the moment he had uttered it. Why, ladies did not wear their finest gown and finest jewels merely to sit at home. *Did they?*

"I am indeed," Catherine said with a smile, pulling one of her gloves to ensure her fingers were taut within the silk.

And she said nothing more. Micah waited for what felt like an eternity, but she appeared to be in no rush to give him extraneous details. It appeared if he wished to know more, he would have to…ask.

"And where are you going?" Micah asked, trying to keep the tension in his shoulders from his voice.

He had not, it seemed, done a very good job. Catherine stared, as though his presence was inexplicable, and only when she had stepped away and back to a small looking glass that was propped up on a bookshelf did she speak.

"The opera."

The opera? Micah's jaw fell open. Why, she could not go to the opera! There were countless men there, cads and rakes the lot of them—none of them would treat her with any respect! Besides, a woman attending the opera on her own, without a guide or chaperone…how on earth did she think she was going to manage it?

But what really stung, even if he had no wish to admit it, was that the idea of Catherine having plans for this evening…of not being here, thinking of him, wondering what he was doing, was abhorrent.

"Micah?"

Micah closed his mouth hurriedly. "Yes?"

"I am no expert, but you look as though you have experienced a great shock," said Catherine conversationally, as she examined her reflection in the looking glass and pinched her cheeks. "As I am sure you have attended the opera at least once, I have to assume you are not confused about where I am going. It only remains to ask what on earth *has* astonished you?"

She turned, and Micah's stomach lurched most painfully.

She was the most beautiful, the most elegant, the most charming...how could he have ignored it for so long? How could he have been so blind, so ignorant of his own feelings?

Whatever they were.

"It did not occur to me that you may have other plans," he blurted.

Catherine merely raised an eyebrow at his words, something that made Micah's whole body tingle. She would immediately cancel now, of course, she would wish to be with him.

Oh, the delights they would experience tonight—

"I see," Catherine said coolly. "Well, you are welcome to stay here if you wish, you can just pull the door to when you leave."

And with that, she started to walk toward the door—she was actually leaving!

Micah acted on instinct. It did not take long for him to step across the room and take her hand in his, and he heard the sudden intake of breath, the way her eyes flashed with desire.

She wanted him—she wanted to stay. All she needed was a sufficient excuse.

"I don't want you to go," Micah said quietly. "You cannot go."

But Catherine had lost none of her boldness, despite what Micah thought he had seen in her eyes. "Lady Romeril's son certainly thinks I can."

Lady Romeril—Lady Romeril's son?

Micah dropped her hand as though he had been burned. Catherine Tetlow and that foppish fool who hardly knew the front end of a horse?

"You cannot be serious."

"Very serious," came back Catherine's quick reply. "He has invited me to the opera, and I have accepted. I may well be late now, but then I believe Lady Romeril favors those who make an entrance."

Micah's jaw clenched. No, this was impossible. He knew envy when he tasted it—had suffered enough of it whenever he found himself pitted against Coral—but this was different. This was not envy, this was jealousy.

He would not share her.

The realization that Catherine stepping out of this room to meet with that cad Romeril could injure him, would injure him, that the very thought would break his heart…

A ricochet of pain across his chest. Micah hardly knew what to do with himself.

He would not be sharing Catherine. Not with anyone. Not ever.

Micah swallowed. *Blast.*

Well, she had been so certain she would win him, and Catherine had evidently seen something in him he had not recognized. This longing to be with her, this desire to spend all the hours of the day with her—a desire for her beyond her physical beauty…

He had never noticed it before, but she had seen it within him, and Catherine had known precisely what it was, even if he had not.

Love.

Micah swallowed again. No, he would not permit himself to fall in love—but then, did a man have any choice? How could he wrench the passion he felt for Catherine from his heart without removing the organ entirely?

"Y-You…you can't go," he breathed.

He had not intended to sound pathetic, but Catherine did not appear repulsed.

To the contrary, despite the fact he no longer had a hold on her, she did not step away. She stepped closer, so close Micah could kiss those cherry red lips if he moved but an inch.

"Why?" Catherine whispered, her eyes dancing as they met his own. "Give me one good reason why."

A frisson of tension rushed down Micah's spine. He knew what he should say; knew what he should tell her, that he had no interest in sharing his mistress with anyone else, and Lady Romeril's sons, the lot of them, it didn't matter which she intended to meet, were complete animals.

Because he could not share what was in his heart. Not to her. Not to anyone.

"Because Lady Romeril's son is a cad."

"You don't even know which one I am meeting."

Damn. "Both are awful."

"The only awful thing they are accused of is bad taste, and I intend to cure him."

"It's cold outside."

"I'll wear a pelisse," said Catherine quietly. "You'll have to do better than that, Micah."

Micah hesitated. He could see that, but it did not seem possible. "Many other reasons."

"Give me one."

She was so close, Micah could almost feel her warmth radiating from the gown. He breathed in her scent, almost groaned at the tantalizing closeness of the woman he…he…

"I can't," Micah said in a cracked voice.

Catherine did not step away, nor berate him. "Why?"

Her question was heartfelt, almost a plea, and Micah dropped his gaze to find she had taken his hand in hers.

The glove had been removed. He had not noticed her doing that, but he was grateful, for the sensation of her skin on his was perhaps the only thing that could prompt him to say the five words he knew she needed to hear.

"Because I care about you."

The words were whispered, almost breathed, but Micah could see she'd heard them.

Her brow softened, and somehow both her hands were entwined in his. "You care about me?"

Micah nodded. *Oh God, so much, so much it hurt...* "Yes."

"Care?"

He swallowed. "I need you. I want you, I cannot—living without you, knowing you're not mine...you have to be mine, Cat. You have to."

"Does this mean you won't be taking any more mistresses?" she asked with a teasing air.

He almost laughed with relief. *More mistresses?* The idea of taking another woman to his bed, of having to pour himself into another...it was abhorrent. It could not be borne, just as he could not permit Catherine to welcome another into her arms.

That was where he belonged. With her, and no other.

"No more mistresses?" he said with a smile, the atmosphere in the room softening as they came, finally, to an understanding. "Where does that leave you then, Cat?"

Catherine leaned forward and kissed him hard on the mouth. Micah almost cried out, for she tasted so sweet and yet so forbidden, their first kiss with this new understanding.

The kiss ended, leaving them both breathless.

"I may be a determined mistress," Catherine exhaled, "but only so I get what I want."

And that was when Micah lost all sense of control.

Why be controlled when the woman he wanted to bed was in his arms, craving his touch? Why hold back when they had finally reached an understanding they could agree on: that they cared for each other, needed each other, wanted each other, that the thought of the other treading outside of this room with a third party was abhorrent.

The silk gown ripped.

"Micah!"

"You want me to stop?" Micah moaned, forcing the silk to the floor, piles of it as Catherine stood in naught but her corset. "Damn woman, you were going to meet him without any underclothes?"

Catherine smiled wickedly as she moved her near-naked form into his arms. "All the better to play with me."

A guttural groan was ripped from Micah's throat as he kissed her hard, her lips parting immediately to welcome him in, and his hands barely knew where to start, where to stop, grazing Catherine's neck, down to her corset, her quivering thighs that led up to—

"Oh no, you don't!"

Micah gasped as he was pushed back, almost stumbling in his haze of desire, but he had no complaint, not as Catherine's eager fingers pulled off his coat, his waistcoat, tugging at his cravat as he hoped she would soon be tugging at his—

"Catherine," he moaned.

No other man would have been unable to withstand it. Ignoring him for a moment, a moment in which Micah ached for her touch, he was at least rewarded with the sight of Catherine pulling at the ties of her corset and dropping it swiftly to the floor.

And there she was, all of her, and Micah fumbled with the buttons of his breeches, wanting to be just as naked as she was, just as ready as she—

"Catherine!"

Micah tilted back his head and moaned. As though she had read his mind, Catherine had dropped to her knees, pulling down his breeches just as his fingers had managed to undo them, and he was inside her, his manhood within that warm welcoming mouth, and he quivered with pleasure as her tongue slowly licked down him.

"Mmm," she moaned.

Micah blinked. It was all he could do to stay standing upright, and though Catherine had kissed him like this before, many times, it was nothing to the newfound intimacy they had shared with their words, and he was going to—

"Catherine!" Micah cried out as his hips took over, thrusting into her mouth as he poured into her.

She lifted her head, eyes blazing with desire.

Trying desperately not to think of just how spent he was going to be after this evening, Micah swept Catherine up in his arms and threw her onto the bed.

"Micah, what are you—"

"I think you deserve a little treat," said Micah, crawling between her legs. "Just stay still."

He had never shared this with Catherine; it was one of the few lines they had never crossed, but as Micah's heart thumped wildly and his body already started to ache with pleasure again, he knew this was what he wanted to do.

He wanted to show her, not just tell her, what Catherine meant to him.

"M-Micah?" stammered Catherine, propping herself up on her elbows as he slowly kissed down her torso, entirely ignoring her breasts. "What are you—Micah!"

Micah almost cried out her name at the same time but managed to stop himself. It would have been rather difficult, after all, with his tongue inside her secret place.

Oh God, and she tasted so good. Hesitantly at first, then with greater strength as Catherine's whimpers echoed around the room, Micah lapped at the sweetness of her inner center.

As his thumb and forefinger tightened around one of Catherine's nipples, Micah darted his tongue deep within her.

"Yes, oh, yes, more, more!"

Micah knew how to obey. As his hand caressed her breast and his tongue turned a delicate circle around the quivering sweet nub within her, one of her hands clutching his hair, keeping him there, he felt her body shiver, the movement increasing as her moans heightened, until—

"Micah!"

Every inch of her shook. Micah was an expert in loving women, and he knew when a woman had lost all control thanks to the ecstasy that swept through her.

He lifted his head. Catherine had lust-hazed eyes.

"That…that was—"

"Only the beginning," breathed Micah, lifting himself up and plunging his ready manhood within her.

Catherine arched her back, her eyelashes fluttering. "I want you—"

"I know," Micah said, kissing her hard on the mouth as he started to echo the rhythm he had built so expertly with his tongue, now with his manhood, cradling her close to him. "Cat, oh, Cat—"

"Micah—"

And it was all he could do to hold himself back for a moment as he built the pleasure within her again. Catherine's hands scrabbled at his back, desperate to hold onto something as she lost all control once again.

"Oh, God!"

And Micah took her cry as permission to lose himself in her, and as he poured himself into her, he knew he could never touch another woman again.

CHAPTER FOURTEEN

November 2, 1812

I
T WAS LATE.

Catherine did not know precisely what time it was, only that she had been awoken by sunlight drifting across her boudoir to reach her bed.

At this time of year, it must be late. Mid-morning. Perhaps nearer noon.

She did not really care. It was warm, and her sheets were soft, and every part of Catherine ached in a sort of delightful happiness she could not quite understand. She recognized it, yes, but so often this moment was filled with sadness.

The morning after.

Micah had been, and Micah had certainly come…and then Micah was gone.

Catherine swallowed, eyes shut, as memories of the evening soared through her mind.

They had laughed, and Catherine had been held by him, really held, and she had known such joy as she had never experienced. It was too much, and not enough, and everything had been leading up to it in her life.

Catherine slowly opened her eyes. Her smile broadened.

And he was still here.

No one else had seen this side of Micah, Catherine thought happily. At least, if he had always behaved with his other mistresses as he had with her, and she had no reason to think any differently, he would normally have slipped away by now.

But today…

"I need you. I want you, I cannot—living without you, knowing you're not mine…you have to be mine, Cat. You have to."

A warm glow spread across Catherine's chest that had nothing to do with lovemaking. He needed her; that was what he had said, and if any gentleman had said that, she would have thought them teasing.

But not Micah.

She had seen it in his eyes, felt it in his fingers, tasted it when she had kissed him.

He loved her.

Catherine smiled. True, he had not said the precise words, but what gentleman did? They were not trained to think of feelings, were they?

Which reminded her. She really must, at some point, have a conversation with John about…well. Love and the like. Though it would be uncomfortable for the both of them, she would have to make sure he—

"You are thinking of something rather serious."

Catherine started, then softened as she saw Micah's smile. He had awoken without her noticing, lost as she had been in her thoughts.

"Micah."

"That's what they call me," he said, groaning as he stretched out. "Only you from now on, though, of course," he said hastily as Catherine opened her eyes in mock horror.

She giggled. "I know that."

In a strange way, Catherine was not entirely sure what to do with herself. This had never happened; they had awoken together once, true, but it had been after no lovemaking the previous evening, no declarations of affection, no demands of exclusivity in their caresses.

And that was precisely what had happened last night.

She had him. Micah de Petras was hers, not just in her bed but in his heart. She had seduced him, finally, body and soul.

"You are looking at me."

Catherine smiled, twisting to lie on her side as she examined him. "So I am."

"I'm not sure how I feel about it, to tell the truth," said Micah with a dry laugh. "It's so...so—"

"Intimate," Catherine supplied.

For a moment, she thought she had gone too far, but he gave her a lopsided grin. "Something like that."

"Well, intimacy would rather be the order of the day, as far as I am concerned," said Catherine, her teasing spirit rising in her as joy in his company overwhelmed her. "After all, what was it you said last night? You cared for me? Needed me, wanted me—"

Micah groaned and turned onto his front to bury his head in the pillow. "I thought you might have forgotten that!"

His voice was muffled but no less coherent, and Catherine giggled as she watched the flush of embarrassment creep across his neck.

As though she could ever forget such a delightful admission!

"Never fear!" Catherine laughed, reaching out and putting her arm around his naked back, stomach lurching at the warmth of his skin. "You think I'd forget that?"

Micah groaned again, and she could not help but laugh, his teasing smile appearing just briefly as he twisted to look at her before he stuck his face once more in the pillow.

Was it possible to be this incandescent with joy? Was it possible to survive after being overwhelmed with such love?

Catherine could hardly breathe, she was so happy. After two long years of doing precisely what was asked of her, of falling in love slowly and despite her best attempts, falling in love with the man who paid her for her body...

"You know," said Micah, turning to face her and propping

himself up on an elbow that gave Catherine a delightful view of his arms, "I rather like this."

Catherine raised an eyebrow. "This?"

He could not have been more vague if he had tried, and Micah seemed to realize he had been unhelpfully imprecise. "This. Waking up together, here. You and me."

"I rather like it, too."

"And you know what these sorts of things can lead to," said Micah, his voice lowering as he pulled Catherine toward him—not that she put up much of a fight.

"I do indeed…"

It was luncheon by the time Catherine managed to persuade Micah to leave her bed.

"But I want to bed you again!"

"And I have just as much desire for that, but my body can take no more until you feed me," said Catherine with a laugh, managing to dart past Micah's wandering hands as she slipped out of the bed. "No, I am serious, Micah! I am hungry!"

"And so am I," said Micah darkly.

She giggled, pulling off a bedsheet to cover herself.

"And you are blocking the most beautiful view, you heartless woman!"

"So are you," Catherine pointed out.

Micah said nothing but pushed all the bedsheets from the bed, revealing himself in all his glory.

Catherine's breath caught in her throat. He really was very handsome, every inch of him—some inches more so than others. But she truly was not being sensational when she said she needed to eat. Why, it had almost been an entire four and twenty hours since she had taken a meal, and if they were to return here this evening for just such a night…

Her heart contracted, skipping a beat with happiness. Because they would, wouldn't they? Why be apart, ever, now that they had found each other?

"You mean to tell me you won't get back into bed with me?"

Catherine laughed at Micah's mock horror. "That is precisely what I am saying."

"Well, there's nothing for it then," came Micah's gleeful retort as he jumped out of bed. "I shall just have to make love to you here—"

"Micah!"

Catherine accepted his kiss as he pressed her against a wall, but then pushed him aside. "I am serious, Micah. I cannot—you have worn me out! Feed me. Let me rest...then I can give you what you want."

Her eyes met his, passionate and serious, and she smiled as she saw him realize she was in earnest.

"Of course—ruffian that I am, I have not kept my woman fed and watered," said Micah with a grin. "Come on!"

Did every woman simply melt when the love of their life described them as 'their woman', or was that a peculiarity only Catherine had? She did not know; could not know, had no one to ask.

All she knew was that as the two of them slowly got dressed—Micah hunting for his cravat, Catherine slipping on a simple cotton muslin gown—there was nowhere else she wanted to be, and no one else she wished to be with.

"Ah," said Micah, picking up the red silk gown he had summarily destroyed the previous evening.

Catherine sighed. "It was a beautiful gown."

"I'll buy you a new one."

"Just the one?" she teased, walking to the looking glass to retrieve some hairpins.

"One for each day of the week," said Micah, throwing himself onto the bed, fully clothed, as he watched her prepare her hair. "Except Thursdays."

Catherine raised an eyebrow as she caught his gaze in the reflection. "Not Thursdays?"

Micah shook his head with a wicked grin. "On those days you shall be naked."

She quivered at the thought. An entire day given over to pleasure. It would have been painful to consider without Micah's admission of affection, but now she knew he loved her…

"Come on then," she said, smoothing her skirts and retrieving her pelisse. "Where are you taking me?"

"No idea in the slightest," declared Micah, offering her his arm. "Shall we?"

Could the world not see how unbelievably happy she was? It was beyond Catherine's belief that every person they passed on the streets of London did not congratulate her.

She had done the impossible—at least, the seemingly impossible.

She had made Micah de Petras fall in love with her.

There was a special kind of pride, walking on Micah de Petras' arm. They had never done this before. Catherine had always welcomed him to her rooms, and that had been the beginning and end of all their encounters.

But as the streets bustled with those who had come to Town for the Season, Catherine saw the envious eyes of many settle on her and Micah as they walked past. They wanted to be her, wanted to be the one walking with him arm in arm, and she could not blame them.

The question was, when would he ask the question that would secure their happiness?

Catherine was not a romantic, at least, she did not consider herself to be. She did not require long speeches, dramatic declarations—she did not even require Micah to have rehearsed the question in advance.

As long as he asked it. As long as he told her in no uncertain terms that he would be bereft without her, and needed her as his bride…

That would be enough.

"Catherine, I have a very important question to ask you," said Micah softly.

Catherine stiffened, but forced herself to relax as they wandered down a street.

"Of—Of course," she replied breathlessly. "You…you can ask me any question you like."

Micah shot her a strange look before pointing out a woman about twenty paces ahead of them. "That woman—there, with the blue gown. Do you recognize her?"

Catherine's heart sank. Well, naturally it was not going to be that simple, and she had been a fool to think he would so recklessly ask such a question of import.

So, he was not going to propose this very moment.

That still left the question of the woman who had caught Micah's eye. Try as she might, Catherine could not help but feel aggrieved to see he appeared more interested in identifying arbitrary women on the street than attend to her.

She cast a careless glance at the woman in question. "No idea."

"Are you sure? She looks remarkably familiar," persisted Micah, craning his neck as the pavement became more crowded.

Catherine swallowed. *There was no harm in looking, of course.* Why, she may one day look at another gentleman and think, within the solitude of her heart, that he was a rather well-formed man and would probably know how to please a woman.

But that did not mean she would be so foolish as to say it!

"Familiar? I would not say so," she said as airily as she could manage. "Why, there must be a hundred women just like her all over the town."

Micah snorted. "You think so?"

Catherine tightened her grip on his arm. "Y-Yes. No. She looks like she could be a Fitzroy."

And in that instant, everything became pain. She could not keep him from other women—how could she? Micah was a man, a gentleman, and with that privilege most doors in London would be open to him. Him, but not her. Though he could go where he pleased, there was nothing to stop him from—

"Huh, that must be why I thought I recognized her," said

Micah as he turned to Catherine with a smile. "Now, food. Do you crave a full meal? If not, there is a coffee house that does most excellent pastries quite close to here that my sister and I used to frequent."

"Which sister?" Catherine managed to ask.

Was it that easy for men? Were they able to so swiftly remove their thoughts of a woman, as though she had not been there in the first place?

"Coral, believe it or not," he said with a short laugh. "Yes, she's sat me down there many a time, hoping to convince me out of…well. Perhaps we should not go there."

Catherine's stomach twisted painfully. She did not need Micah to complete his sentence to know precisely what he was going to say.

So, Coral de Petras, the eldest of the siblings and the one who would one day be the head of the family…she disapproved of Catherine? Of all Micah's mistresses, probably, she was certainly not special.

Marry Micah? Of course she wanted to, more than anything. To be his bride, to be his wife, to spend each day of their future beside him…

It was all she wanted.

But Micah had mentioned nothing of marriage or any sort of commitment beyond the next meal. And what if his family decided against her? Despite what Micah said, he cared about his family, all of them, cared about their opinions. What could a gentleman who was not the heir do against such weighty opposition?

"Cat? Catherine?"

Catherine started. Micah was looking at her closely, concern across his face.

Attempting to smile, she said, "It's nothing."

"It's not nothing," Micah said quietly. "I know you, Catherine. I know all about you, every inch of you—and when I say that, I mean I know your expressions. The way your eyes crinkle when you laugh, that little line you get between your eyes when you're about to say something you know won't be met well."

"Something that happens all too often," she said as they stepped across the street, narrowly avoiding a carriage. Why, the last time she had seen Mary—

"So, when I say it's not nothing, I say so advisedly," Micah said. "Tell me."

Catherine swallowed. This was not the place for this sort of conversation. In truth, she was not sure what was.

"I am hungry, that is all," Catherine said, forcing a smile on her face and realizing to her surprise that some of the discomfort in her stomach truly was hunger. "Feed me, Micah. Then I may be a little more reasonable."

He snorted as they continued down the pavement and stopped outside one of the finest French patisseries in the city. "I doubt that very much. Well then. Three cakes or five?"

CHAPTER FIFTEEN

November 3, 1812

ONLY WHEN ONE of the candles went out did Micah notice he was still sitting there.

Right where he had started, hours ago, when his dinner had been warm. Brought to him by Holland, Micah had played with it a while, stomach growling but heart not in it. As he looked down at the cold fish, his stomach turned. He could not eat that. Not while his mind was fixed on other things.

"Damn," he breathed out slowly.

Well, he had done the best he could. He had tried to hold out, tried to convince himself it would never happen. Why, he had been certain he would not be so easily caught!

He seemed to recall that he had made a rather bold statement to that effect.

"Cat, I am sorry to say that I can guarantee you cannot."

A smile crept across his face. Well, he would not be the first fool to fall in love, and he would certainly not be the last—but he might just be the first fool to fall in love with his mistress, after denying it would even be possible.

He would just have to admit it, there was nothing else for it.

He had almost done so anyway, after all.

"I need you. I want you, I cannot—living without you, knowing

you're not mine...you have to be mine, Cat. You have to."

Micah closed his eyes for a moment, cringing at his words. Why had he not just come out and said it? Why had he been so cryptic, when it had been perfectly clear in Catherine's smile that she knew precisely what he meant?

Catherine.

Just the thought of her was enough to make his heart patter like a green-gilled fool, and Micah groaned aloud.

He was in love with her.

In *love*. Completely in love, so in love, it was getting difficult to concentrate on anything else. He had been hungry when Holland had brought the food, but now he could think of nothing but her. Food had completely fallen by the wayside.

And if he was not careful, he was going to...

"Damn," Micah repeated aloud.

The word echoed around the room, but it did not change his heart's desire.

Catherine. All of her, all the time. Matrimony, precisely what Micah had been determined to avoid. Oh, his family was going to crow about this...

The bellpull by the fireplace had worn thin in a few places, Micah noticed as he reached out for it. He would have to let the man know.

Within a minute, the manservant who serviced the lodgers appeared. "You rang, sir."

"I did indeed," said Micah. "You have my rent for the next quarter in advance, and I wish for you to take one hundred pounds and have it sent to Miss Catherine Tetlow, of Parson's Buildings."

"One of your mistresses, I presume?"

It was all Micah could do not to grin. Yes, it was a presumption now. What was Catherine to him? Lover? Something more than that, yet he had not asked her the question that would place her firmly within his life for the rest of hers.

Something he would have to rectify swiftly.

"Yes, something like that," Micah said aloud. "I lost a wager."

"I will make you fall in love with me."

"Cat, I am sorry to say that I can guarantee you cannot."

And goodness, hadn't he lost it? Micah could still remember the confidence which had surged through his body when he had uttered those words. It had been incomprehensible to him at the time, the idea of handing over one's heart, of making oneself so vulnerable to another.

But when that other was Catherine…

In a way, he was impressed she had managed it. After all, he had been bedding her for what—nigh on two years? And at no point had he ever conceived of her as anything more than a pleasant mistress. One to keep, certainly, but not one to wed.

The manservant cleared his throat. "Sir?"

Micah jerked up his head. "What?"

He really should try to attend. It was starting to become a concern, this inability to think of anything except Catherine, even when she was not in the room.

"I was asking, sir, whether there was anything else I could get you," repeated Holland with a rather severe expression. "I see the dinner I prepared for you was unsatisfactory."

Micah glanced back at his plate.

"The food was excellent, it was my stomach that was unsatisfactory," he said aloud, ashamed at having wasted good food. "Feel free to take it away, Holland, I'll have nothing else this evening."

The man bowed, evidently disappointed at the lack of appreciation for his cooking, and was soon out of the room.

Micah leaned back in his chair and sighed, the one remaining candle fluttering.

He had expected once he fell in love—if he was so foolish as to permit such a thing to happen—that he would be devastated. That his life would be over, that all freedom and choice would be wrenched from him.

But as the memory of Catherine laughing at him just a few

days ago, cream on his nose from one of the cakes he had bought them, Micah felt only warmth, joy, and...hope.

Hope. Hope for the future.

Micah shifted in his chair, suddenly finding it far less comfortable. When had he lost hope in the future, exactly? Was it when he had first realized it would be Coral, and not himself, who would be inheriting?

Was it when Coral had married, and his parents had the audacity to inform him that because old Glaenarm was wealthy, Coral had given back her dowry which would now form part of his own?

His dowry! The outrage!

But now, with Catherine by his side just as often as she was in his bed...now he could consider the future with a smile. With hope. With joyful expectation of laughter, pleasure, and that strange satisfying sensation in one's gut when all was right with the world.

Most disconcerting.

But that would mean, Micah knew, that he had to do something about it. One could not merely step into this form of happiness into wedded bliss without a few formalities.

No matter how repugnant they had once seemed to him.

Standing and stretching out his arms, Micah breathed a heavy yet contented sigh. His world had been seeped in bitterness for too long. Bitterness had overcome him, but it was time to build something different. Build something...with Catherine.

"Damn it all," said Micah, hanging his head. "I'm going to have to talk to my mother."

The night had drawn in early, but he was certain the de Petras family would be at home.

The streets were cold. Micah stamped along them, trying to keep feeling in his toes as he marched toward his parents' home. There was a light upstairs, where the parlor and drawing room were; the parlor at the front of the house, overlooking the street, had its curtains closed but there was most definitely light there.

He hesitated on the doorstep only for a moment. He was doing the right thing; the right thing for himself and Catherine. The fact that it would greatly delight his parents was neither here nor there.

As much as he disliked proving his family right—and they were not right on this occasion, it was complete chance he had fallen so deeply, so irrevocably in love with Catherine—he had to face them.

Had to hear the taunts, the crowing of his sisters—*oh, Lord, Sapphire was going to be disgusting!*

Catherine's face soared into Micah's mind. He smiled and knocked on the door.

It would all be worth it. All for her.

Mrs. Clarkson raised her eyebrows as she opened the door. "Master Micah. You were not expected."

"Hullo, Clarkson," said Micah with a rueful smile. She had never liked him much. "Are my parents within?"

"They are certainly not without," came the clipped response.

It was all he could do not to snap at the woman. Really, he was not a child anymore!

"In that case, I will thank you for not announcing me," Micah said unceremoniously, pushing past the housekeeper into the familiar hallway. "I know the way."

She sniffed in response.

Micah's stomach lurched as he placed his greatcoat on the hook beside his father's. True, he usually only visited unannounced when he needed money…and in a way one could consider this visit much in the same vein…

But it was different, wasn't it?

He hesitated even longer outside the parlor. He could hear laughter inside; the quiet laughter of people who had known each other far too long to quarrel.

Micah's heart skipped a beat. Would he and Catherine be like that one day? Settled around a fire, gentle conversation washing over them as they bickered good-naturedly about whether to order chicken or salmon for dinner the next day?

He opened the door.

"Micah!"

"Son, how pleasant to see you!"

"Is Maltravers with you?"

Micah blinked in the sudden brightness of the parlor after the darkness of the hall and laughed dryly at Sapphire's immediate request. "I don't keep James in my pocket, Sapphy."

His sister was curled up in an armchair, a book in her hands. "You two are so frequently together, I rather assumed you come as a pair."

"Is this the earl?" asked Amethyst, leaning forward with interest.

Micah saw a flicker of something that could be irritation in his sister's expression. Now, where had that come from?

"If anyone is a pair with Maltravers, it is you, Sapphy," pointed out their mother. "You never left that boy alone when you were little, always running after—"

"Mama! I am seventeen years of age, I hardly run after anyone!" protested Sapphire.

Micah closed the door behind him and took in the scene. His father appeared to be puzzling through a newspaper at one end of the sofa while his mother sat nearer the fire, evidently trying to draw Sapphire into a conversation. Amethyst was, as usual, seated on her own.

Not that that mattered now. Opal was positively beaming at her son, though Micah could see a frown of concern starting to crease his father's forehead.

"Micah, I did not expect you, I would have kept some dinner back—you have eaten?"

"Yes," Micah lied automatically. Mrs. Clarkson had enough of a reason to dislike him without forcing her back into the kitchen. "Mama, I—"

"I heard you danced with a young lady at Penshaw's ball, you know," said Opal, patting the vacant chair opposite her and grinning. "I want to hear all about her!"

A weak smile grazed Micah's lips. He doubted very much his mother actually wanted to hear all about her. There were certain things one could never say to their parents, no matter how understanding or interested they were.

But the first thing he needed to do was remove Sapphire.

"Sapphy," he said easily, throwing himself into the suggested seat. "Go away."

Sapphire's eyes widened. "Of all the rude, inconsiderate—"

"Please, Sapphy."

If anything, that last pronouncement only made her eyes widen further. Micah so rarely spoke softly to his sisters, there was often, in his opinion, little cause to.

After all, Emerald usually said nothing, Sapphire often spoke nonsense, and anything Coral uttered could be safely ignored.

Sapphire opened her mouth, closed it, then glanced at her mother. Opal nodded.

Micah felt his shoulders relax as he watched his sister rise.

"Fine," she said succinctly, tucking her book under her arm. "I'll take the carriage, Mama, and go and see Maltravers."

"At this time?" Jasper's voice was all astonishment, and Micah could not blame him. *The brazenness of the girl!* "Sapphire de Petras, you'll gain yourself a reputation—"

"Oh, Maltravers does not count," Sapphire said, waving her arms as she reached the door. "He won't mind. I'll be back within the hour, Mama. Sleep tight."

And with that, she was gone.

"And you, too, Amethyst, if you do not mind," said Micah a little more awkwardly.

Well, he hardly knew the woman, but he was certain he did not wish to have this conversation before her. He did not really wish to have the conversation in the first place.

"Me?" Amethyst looked astonished. "Why?"

"Yes, why, Micah?" asked his mother pointedly.

Micah sighed. "I wish to speak to my parents alone, Amethyst, I am sure you can understand—"

"Am I not part of this family?" Amethyst said immediately, nostrils flaring.

It was all he could do not to snap at her. "Well, you have not acted like it for most of your time here!"

"Micah!"

That was his father, but Micah could no longer hold back. They could not tiptoe around this interloper any longer. "Why are you here, Amethyst? For my parents' money? Because—"

"Because I have nowhere else to go!" Amethyst flushed as she spoke. "Because my parents are gone, as you well know, and I have nowhere...my father was awful! You have no idea, the safety you have in your family, the love, the welcome..."

Her voice trailed away as her throat became choked, her eyes filling with tears.

Oh, blast. Micah had not intended this, not at all, but now he'd done it.

Opal rose and sat beside her niece, her hand clasping the younger woman's. "We have never prevented you from being a part of this family, you know. You have held yourself aloft from us, made it difficult for us to—"

"I've never really been a part of a family before," Amethyst said in a low voice. "Never known what it was to...well."

"I am sorry, Amethyst," Micah said. "I did not mean—"

"I know." She sniffed and looked up with bright eyes but a brave smile. "I will leave you to discuss whatever it is with your parents. I am sure you have much to talk about."

All eyes watched Amethyst as she rose, disentangling her hand from Opal's, and stepped around the sofa. The door closed quietly behind her.

Micah took a deep breath. Now he was alone with his parents, the conversation that he intended to have felt rather uncomfortably real. Once he said these words aloud, there would be no way back. No way out.

To his intense surprise, Micah discovered he did not want

one.

"Well, Micah," said Jasper quietly, putting down his newspaper and looking at his son with apprehension painted across his face. "You wished to speak to us."

Micah could see the panic in his parents, controlled yes, but under the surface. The only other time he had sat them down like this, it had been to inform them of a rather large gambling debt he had accrued at the races.

"I need to talk about money," Micah began.

Damn. Now why had he slipped into old habits! That really wasn't what he wanted to talk about at all—not really!

"Money. Of course you do, Micah, I should not have expected anything else. Whom to and how much?" his mother asked.

Micah swallowed. It was a little galling to see his parents had such little faith in him, but in a way, he supposed it was for the best. He would be able to surprise them, perhaps for the first time in a positive way, and show them he was not so useless as they thought.

Probably.

"It's not like that," he said hastily. "It's about...well. I am apportioned an income from your estate, Mama—"

"The rentals in Bath," Opal nodded. "Yes. They are not delivering sufficiently for you? Just how much is your lodging per month, anyway?"

"That's not what I want to—"

"Because I am certain I could find you cheaper and better rooms, you know," his mother continued, completely ignoring him. "There are such lovely places close to us, in fact, I heard Mrs. Howarth mention her son—"

"Mama," said Micah firmly.

He had to get a grip of this conversation—*on himself*—or else he was likely to leave here with nothing at all.

"Micah," said Opal with a wry smile.

He swallowed. If only he had thought for more than two

minutes about this conversation. There was surely a phrase he could use here to explain everything, to help them to understand…to make them pleased to hear his news!

"Papa," said Micah, turning to his father.

Jasper's eyes widened. "Yes?"

"I…well. I wondered whether…you mentioned in the past that you would one day sign over half the shipping business to me."

Micah could not understand why there was such a look of astonishment on his father's face. It had not been his suggestion in the first place, after all, and Jasper had spoken of it as though it was a certainty, even if it had not precisely been…done.

"Indeed, I did say that," said Jasper quietly. "But there were conditions attached to that, if you remember. Establishing yourself within the business, giving you an independent income, those were only to happen when—"

"Micah de Petras, you know we intended you to have that when you were married!" said Opal crossly. Two pink dots had appeared on her cheeks. "Do you delight in vexing me, or it is completely by chance that you are able to singularly—"

"I thought you could consider it…my dowry."

The instant the words were out of his mouth, Micah held his breath. The moment his parents realized what he was saying, what he was actually saying, there would be dancing in the streets.

Jasper's mouth was hanging open.

Micah waited, but his father did not appear to have any words. A tad prickled, he turned to his mother.

Opal was frowning. Her mouth was not open, her jaw tightly clenched, and a nerve throbbed at her temple.

Micah could not understand it. Were they not happy for him? Had they not been badgering him for goodness knows how long, to pick a bride and settle down?

What more could they possibly want from him?

"Now, Micah, that is unkind," said Jasper quietly.

It was Micah's turn for his jaw to drop. "Unkind?"

"You know your mother and I have great hopes for your happiness in that quarter, and we do not take kindly to being teased," said Jasper as he took his wife's hand in his. "I think you should apologize to your mother."

"But I—Mama, I am in earnest!" Micah protested. He almost laughed, it was so ridiculous. *They did not believe him?* "I could not bring her here tonight. I am unable to propose until I know just whether I can support—"

"You mean to say you've found someone?" interrupted Opal, all astonishment. "Someone you…you actually wish to marry?"

Micah swallowed. *Someone he wanted to marry.* Someone he could not live without, someone who consumed him, body and soul. Someone who was, at any moment this evening, receiving one hundred pounds as the winner of a wager for his heart.

"Yes," he said quietly.

"And—and you think she will marry you?" asked his mother, still evidently amazed that there was such a person in the world. "She loves you, you mean?"

"Loves me?" Micah took a deep breath, hands twisting in his lap as he considered.

Catherine, love him?

There was certainly no other explanation for it all. Why she had concocted the wager in the first place, why she had been so determined to make him choose her above all other mistresses. And only now did Micah wonder whether Catherine had purposefully attended that damned ball of Penshaw's, whether her teasing with that dratted Mr. Lister and whichever one of Lady Romeril's sons she was attending the opera with was all…

A slow smile crept across Micah's lips. *Well, she had said she would have him. And she was right.*

"Yes," he said quietly. "I love her, and she loves me. All I need now is sufficient funds to buy a home, offer us an income, and—"

"Live," said Opal with a misty-eyed smile. "Happily ever after."

CHAPTER SIXTEEN

November 6, 1812

T HE FIRE CRACKLED and the toast burned, but Catherine did not mind. She liked it that way. Gave the bread more flavor; at least, that was what she always thought.

It had been her mother who had first said that to her. In hindsight, Catherine was almost certain the only reason her mother had uttered such a sentiment was to make Catherine feel better about burning the toast so often.

But over the years, she had rather got a taste for it.

Catherine gingerly pulled the almost black bread from the toasting fork, slathered it in the last of the marmalade—no butter in the house, as she had given most of her funds to Mrs. McCall—and took a hot, sticky mouthful.

She sighed happily. Yes, it was not perhaps the best fare; but it would not be long before she and Micah had a home of their own. A kitchen of their own—perhaps a cook! The idea of someone else cooking, of having full, hot meals, of there always being butter available, even cold perhaps…it was a heady thought.

Catherine smiled as she stuck her last piece of bread onto the toasting fork. Now they had come to a proper understanding, there was no knowing what they may share in the future. A home in London, a home in the country, perhaps?

Happiness, laughter, and joy for the rest of their—

"Yes?"

Catherine turned to the door, her toast almost burned just enough on each side as a knock rang through the room.

It was most odd. She was not expecting anyone, though in truth, the only people who frequented her rooms were Micah, sometimes Mrs. Goldsmith, and on one occasion which had caused her heart to flutter in panic at her sudden appearance, Mrs. McCall.

It had turned out in the end that Mrs. McCall only wished to ascertain if she could have additional funds for a new gown for Mary, but it had caused Catherine great consternation.

However, none of them appeared.

The door opened to reveal a man she vaguely recognized but could not place. "Miss."

Catherine rose, suddenly conscious the gown she was wearing had a dirty hem from the street outside, and she had unpinned her hair in what she had thought was the privacy of the evening.

But the man did not appear interested in her apparel. He held out a letter. "For you."

Catherine blinked. *Post?*

But the man did not look like the postman she knew. Indeed, though he was smartly dressed, it was in no livery or uniform she recognized.

Yet, she had seen the man before, Catherine was sure. Somewhere in the back of her mind was a memory of him, just a snippet, but it was there nonetheless.

"Miss?"

"Wh—Oh, yes," Catherine said hastily, stepping forward to accept the letter.

It appeared the man had no wish to step too far into her rooms, and she could hardly blame him. They were quite obviously those of a woman more than a little down on her luck, and if he was a man of honor, or worse, a gentleman—

"Thank you, Miss," the man said curtly as she took the letter.

After a nod, which could have been a bow, he departed, closing the door.

Catherine blinked after him. How very strange. Not to announce himself, that is, to leave no name, no indication of whom the letter was from. The hand on the front, now she came to examine it, was unknown to her.

What could it be? Only bad news. When she had been young, when her parents had still been alive, good news was brought in person. Only bad news was consigned to a letter.

A spark, just out of the corner of her eye. Catherine whirled around and attempted to rescue the toast now more flame than bread, but it was no use.

She allowed the charcoaled remains to fall into the fire and sighed. Her last piece of bread, too.

Settling herself in the armchair, grateful at least she had enough coal to keep a fire going, Catherine looked once more at the letter. Well, there were no more clues to be gained by examining the outside.

The hand was bold but unknown to her, the paper just as one would expect. It was sealed, but with no mark to identify its sender. Catherine slowly slipped a finger under the seal, breaking it, and opened up the letter.

There were two things within it.

Firstly, a short note. It said:

From the lodgings of Micah de Petras.

And beside it, folded carefully three times...was a ten-pound note.

Ten pounds. Ten pounds? Her going weekly rate, what he paid her for her body, nothing more?

Ten pounds?

Why on earth had Micah sent her ten pounds? It was an insult, a mockery of what they had shared—a pointed reminder she was his dependent, a mistress, and nothing more.

Catherine lifted the ten-pound note to the light, just to check she was not dreaming. No, she was not dreaming. Surely this must be a nightmare, a terrible nightmare she would wake from at any moment.

The paper was soft under her fingertips. It was certainly real.

Catherine turned back to the letter, if one could call it a letter. Now that she looked at it more closely, it was clear it was not in Micah's hand. She'd not had many occasions to see his handwriting, of course, but it was distinctive enough to know this was not it.

He had not even written the note.

She turned it over, heart leaping for a moment as she convinced herself there must be more on the other side; something, anything to explain why he had done this thing.

The paper was blank on the other side.

Catherine raised a hand to her chest as it spasmed in pain, her lungs tight, nothing making sense. Was this what a broken heart felt like?

After all they had shared together. After the years of intimacy and their recent affection. After admitting to each other how much they cared, after he told her…

Catherine swallowed and tried hard to recall precisely what Micah had said.

"I need you. I want you, I cannot—living without you, knowing you're not mine…you have to be mine, Cat. You have to."

The fire crackled, and her heart continued to struggle. He had not actually…well, it was only now she realized Micah had not actually spoken any words of love.

Needed her?

She needed many things, many people—but she did not wish to marry them!

For the first time since she and Micah had, Catherine believed, exchanged their affection, a sliver of ice sank into her heart.

Needed her. Wanted her. It was something one could say so easily, without any momentum behind it, any true feeling. Any genuine heart.

She looked at the ten-pound note. Ten pounds. Her value for one night.

But now…though it was still a significant amount of money, it cheapened her. Was that truly all she was worth? No declarations of love, no wedding ring, no bells as they emerged as husband and wife?

Catherine swallowed. She simply would have to accept her attempt to win Micah's heart, though she had believed herself for a time successful, had utterly failed.

"I will make you fall in love with me."

"Cat, I am sorry to say that I can guarantee you cannot."

A sad smile curled her lips. Well, he had warned her, had he not? Micah had been absolutely certain it would be impossible to make him love her, and for all her arrogance, all her attempts, all the wiles and seductive techniques she had attempted…he had been right.

Micah de Petras had not fallen in love with her.

How long Catherine sat there, she was not sure. It must have been an hour. The fire had died down and weak sunlight poured through the windows before she recollected herself.

Had she slept?

She rubbed at her eyes, aching with tears unshed, still unsure whether slumber had caught her for a few hours in the night. She certainly felt as though she had not slept in days, but that was the ache of her heart.

She could not sit here wasting away after a man who had given her little thought since she had last seen him.

It took her only a moment to find a pencil. It took longer to find paper, eventually, Catherine gave up and decided to simply use the note that had been sent. She may as well make some use of it.

From the lodgings of ~~Micah de Petras.~~ Catherine Tetlow

Catherine looked carefully at it. It was clear enough, wasn't it?

She turned the paper inside out, and carefully printed Mrs. McCall's name and address. She had no wax to make a seal, but some leftover string from the vegetables she had purchased a few days ago sufficed to keep the thing intact.

Catherine breathed in slowly. *There.* The ten pounds would go directly to the people who needed it the most—her siblings. John and Mary would have another half a month secured, and that would give her breathing room to…

But that wasn't enough, was it?

Catherine bit her lip. It was Friday. That meant that in six days' time, Micah would be appearing at her door, assuming they would be continuing their affair. That she would still be his mistress, after everything he had done to her.

A frown creased her forehead. Well, he was very much mistaken.

This time she did continue searching for paper until she found some. It was the end of a bill, true, but she ripped off the top and there was still sufficient room for the short message she needed to send.

Catherine spent far too long considering precisely what had to be said. After all, one only had a few lines, and she wanted to be absolutely clear. Cold, distant, and direct.

Eventually, she settled on:

Micah—I do not wish to see you again. Our arrangement is at an end. C. Tetlow

No matter how she examined it, she could not see any way in which Micah could misunderstand. *And after all,* Catherine told herself, *he was the one who sent her the ten-pound note.* He would surely understand she could not suffer being treated in such a way any longer.

Which left only one problem…

She sighed as she looked around the room. One of only two she had taken. The rent was low, yes, but it was not nothing. She would need to find another...protector, if she was going to continue here and support her siblings.

Another lover. No, that was not the right word, was it? Catherine swallowed. Love was something she would have to avoid, at all costs.

Her mind raced through the few gentlemen she knew who may have both the funds and a lack of mistress. Mr. Lister was absolutely out of the question, he was most irritating, and after careful questions, she had discovered his wealth far lower than what she required.

Lady Romeril's son may do, but then she had heard whispers about himself and Miss Tilney. She could not compete with a courtesan of that elegance. There was no point in attempting that.

Then a name surfaced, one which Catherine had momentarily forgotten, but his face appeared as clear and grinning as she had last seen it.

A quick toilette, a change into a fresh gown, and a hurried conversation with Mrs. Goldsmith who appeared to know everyone in London, and Catherine was ready. She had stepped out into the street, the early hour still freezing, and walked hurriedly along until she reached his townhouse.

Catherine stared, wide-eyed. She had assumed he was wealthier than Micah, but the entire building? She would certainly be well provided for if she could seduce him...

The door was opened by a stern looking butler. "Yes?"

Catherine did not smile. That was what people attempting to ingratiate themselves did, and she had to pretend to be a lady. A lady who would be imperious.

"He is expecting me," she said languidly. "Thank you." She did not wait for a reply, stepping past the butler with that surety of rank she had seen so often. "Where is he?"

"He—his lordship is in the morning room," said the butler, taking her pelisse obediently and pointing to a room leading off the hall. "Who shall I say is—"

"No need to announce me," said Catherine with a nod of her head. "Thank you."

The dismissal was abrupt, but completely in keeping with the way Catherine had seen duchesses speak to their staff, and it appeared she had managed the cadence precisely right.

The butler bowed, evidently considering her to be a far more important personage than she was, and disappeared.

Only then did Catherine permit herself to notice her heart was beating so frantically, it was almost impossible to individually mark out the beats. *This was it.* She had come this far and was determined to continue.

Despite the instinct to knock, Catherine swept into the morning room. "My lord."

James Gresley, Earl of Maltravers, rose hurriedly from his armchair and almost dropped his newspaper. "What the—"

"I assume you do not remember me, and that is entirely my fault for not making a strong enough impression," said Catherine swiftly. *The fewer questions, the better.* "Let me make it perfectly clear why I have come."

It took but four steps to reach him, but with every one she took, Catherine's heart rebelled. She could not do this, she must not do this, even if her siblings needed her money she could not—

Catherine kissed the earl on the lips. She tried to pour as much passion into it as possible, trying to think of Micah, of the connection they had shared, of the intimacy she had won from him.

The kiss ended. Catherine stepped back to see a rather shocked earl, blinking as though she had dazzled him with a candle in the dead of night.

She found, rather to her surprise, that she was breathless. "I-I offer myself to you as a mistress, my lord."

Was that enough? Catherine waited, desperately hoping she had said enough to explain the situation to the man, but he still looked as though he was battling the surprise of her appearance.

She had never given herself to any other man than Micah; had been grateful, for almost the whole two years, that it had been him when it could have been anyone else.

But earls had mistresses all the time, did they not? He would understand, this Maltravers. *Wouldn't he?*

"I…I do not understand—"

"Then let me explain again," said Catherine, stepping forward.

Her intended kiss never occurred. Before she could reach his lips, the earl dropped the newspaper and held onto her arms, holding her about three inches from him.

His gaze caught hers. "No."

She slumped in his grasp, her shoulders falling and her heart sinking. Perhaps she was less alluring than she imagined; perhaps Micah had inelegant tastes. She had coiffed her hair as carefully as she could manage, had borrowed some lip rouge from Mrs. Goldsmith—

"Am I that repulsive?" Catherine sighed heavily.

She had been unable to stop herself from asking the question, and in reply, the earl released her with a shake of his head.

"No," he said quietly. "No, not at all."

"Then why do you refuse me so swiftly?" Catherine asked quietly.

"You are very beautiful," the earl said softly. "It's not…I…"

And Catherine took a closer look—really looked. And she saw it there, almost as though it was written for her to discover. The flush, the darting eyes, the tightened breathing, the desperation and misery on his face…

"Oh, Lord," she said heavily. "You're in love."

"Not with you!" he said hastily.

Catherine laughed as she took a step back. "I rather guessed that. Who is she?"

The gentleman sat heavily in the armchair and put his head in his hands. "It doesn't matter. She would never…she will never consider me that way. It is something I have come to accept, even if it tears me apart."

About a foot behind her was a sofa, and Catherine lowered herself onto it slowly as she took in the sight of the broken man.

Well, this was certainly not what she had expected—but perhaps she should have done. The Earl of Maltravers with no wife, no mistresses…and no indiscretions with gentlemen.

She should have guessed. He was in love, unrequited love. How well she knew the misery.

"I am sorry," she said quietly.

The earl looked up with a desperate smile. "Don't be. I have a feeling you understand me completely."

Catherine nodded and tried to swallow back the tears that threatened, finally, to fall. "If only all men fell in love as willingly as you."

CHAPTER SEVENTEEN

November 7, 1812

Micah sank heavily onto the chair and glowered up at his mother. "Well?"

He could see what she wanted to say in reply. They shared a similar temper, after all, and the words 'well what?' were just on the tip of her tongue.

Opal de Petras, however, clearly had better self-control than her son. She smiled genially from where she was standing by the fire. "I am very well, thank you, Micah."

Micah snorted. Well, his temper had been pushed to the limit with this summons he had received from his mother not half an hour ago. There he had been, just about to depart his lodgings to see Catherine, the one person in the whole world he actually wanted to see…and his mother's note had arrived.

He pulled it out to wave at her. "Well?"

"I don't know why you are so irritable today, Micah," said Sapphire with a smile from the window seat where she had perched. "I know how much you enjoy returning to see us all."

Amethyst giggled, curled up in an armchair.

Micah sniffed, but did not say anything. He was not going to say aloud just how tedious he often found his visits. Not with Coral in the room.

"Well, I must say, you are fortunate Lady Galcrest did not mind me abandoning her in my blue drawing room," said Coral imperiously, as though it would have been far less of an affront if she had been able to leave her guest in an entirely different drawing room. "What on earth is this all about, Mama?"

Micah cast his older sister a glance. It was all an act, surely. Their mother did almost nothing without informing Coral, as the heir to the family.

Emerald was looking at her, too.

"I am sure your friend will understand," came a gentle voice.

That was their father. Micah watched Jasper clasp and unclasp his hands, and a prickle of discomfort twisted his stomach.

This felt serious, whatever it was, though he could not fathom what would be so important as to bring the entire de Petras family together.

After all, what could concern him just as much as Coral? Why was Amethyst still here, she was only a cousin. More, why did Sapphire have to listen? She was still a…

But no. Now Micah came to look at her, dark hair pinned up and bright sparkling eyes, he had to admit Sapphire was no baby, even if he thought of her as such. She was a woman now.

"So, why did you call us all here, Mama?" Coral continued, her gaze fixed on their mother. "It must be rather urgent if it cannot wait until Saturday."

Micah glanced around. "Saturday?"

What had he missed now? And why did Emerald look remarkably uncomfortable?

"It is just…we are having dinner on Saturday," she said quietly.

Micah blinked. "Are we?"

"Not you," said Coral pointedly, tilting her chin up. "The rest of us."

"You never wanted to come, so we stopped inviting you," said Sapphire succinctly.

"Sapphy, that is not quite—"

"Don't say it like that!"

Micah's two other sisters protested instantly, but he could see the truth in their faces, see it in the embarrassment on Amethyst's face. He had irritated them so many times they did not wish to be in his presence anymore.

He had not expected it to hurt, even though it did make sense.

"Let's not talk about that now," said Opal hastily. "I asked you here for a different reason."

Micah's attention snapped back to his mother. Thoughts of Catherine would, unfortunately, have to wait. Though he ached to see her, there was clearly something intriguing happening in the de Petras family.

He glanced at his father, who had tangled his fingers in his lap. Sharp discomfort rocked Micah's heart. If his father, unflappable, always calm in a crisis, was feeling worried…

"Is it about your wills?" asked Coral directly.

Micah snorted. *Trust Coral to be so direct.*

"Yes, and in a way no," said Opal. "Goodness, I did not think this would be difficult to…"

Micah and Sapphire exchanged glances. *Difficult?*

"But why would you change your wills?" Coral asked. "Because of Amethyst?"

Despite himself, Micah looked around at his cousin and noticed all his siblings had done the same. Amethyst flushed under the combined weight of their looks.

"I thought you would have told Coral."

The words had spilled from his mouth before he was able to stop them, but Opal did not look offended. To the contrary, she smiled ruefully.

"This was something that, until we were sure…until I was sure, I suppose," their mother said with a heavy sigh. "It was all so complicated, and in a way, so long ago…"

Micah leaned forward in his chair. Long ago? There had always been rumors; whispers, gossip, a hint of scandal. His mother had always pushed it aside, told her children there was no truth whatsoever in the nonsense, and they should completely ignore anything they heard about her. When Amethyst had arrived, it had become almost more difficult to ask.

It appeared all his siblings were intrigued. Emerald, at least, looked embarrassed, but then she often did in uncomfortable situations, whether it was anything to do with her or not.

Opal took a deep breath. "It was all so long ago. Twenty years? No, more, for it was before I met your father."

Micah glanced at his father. Jasper was now pressing his fingers to his mouth, as though preventing himself from speaking. Amethyst looked pale.

What was going on?

"I have not spoken much about my family—you are my family now, I have not really felt the need to," said Opal. "But years ago, when…when my brother was the head of the de Petras family—"

"My father," Amethyst interrupted.

Micah watched as his mother hesitated, just for a moment, and then nodded. "He was not a good man, as I think anyone who met him would agree. It was my parents' decision to honor the de Petras tradition of the eldest daughter inheriting, but my brother—"

"I cannot imagine my father appreciating that."

Micah glanced at his cousin. She was pale but still resolute. As though she had finally come to accept her father's mistakes, his weakness. Even though it clearly pained her.

Opal took another deep breath. "It never sat well with me, for my parents left him nothing, not a single penny. And now, with his daughter here…well, it seemed like the perfect time to make restitution."

"Here, here," said Jasper quietly.

His parents clasped hands for a moment, only a moment, but evidently, it gave Micah's mother strength to continue. "And that is why I—we have changed our wills. To include Amethyst."

"To include Amethyst?" repeated Coral in horror.

"To include me?" Amethyst said, wide-eyed. "But—I know I asked for—"

"Yes, you did," Coral said darkly. "You arrived here and demanded—"

"But I did not know, I did not understand—there is so much more I value now," Amethyst said hurriedly.

Micah glanced at Sapphire, who looked intrigued, and Emerald, whose face was flushed at the sound of the argument.

Well, so Amethyst would become a de Petras in every way. Not a surprise really, she had been here a year, but evidently Coral did not approve.

"—did not think to discuss this with me?" she was saying to their parents. "I am your heir, after all, and—"

"I'm sorry, m'lady, but this just came for young Master Micah."

The entire family whirled around. Micah glared at Mrs. Clarkson standing in the door holding a note.

Could she have chosen a more inopportune time? Could she not have waited just one minute so they could attempt to untangle this new paradigm his mother had chosen for them?

"Give it to him then," said Opal quietly.

Micah turned back to his mother, desperate to tell her he had no interest in any note.

"Take it, Micah," said his father gruffly.

Micah blinked. Mrs. Clarkson was before him, offering the note with bad grace.

"Thank you," he muttered with equally poor grace, taking the note. "That will be all."

It clearly galled the housekeeper to be so dismissed. She left, snapping the door behind her far louder than it required.

"What does it say, Micah?" Opal said quietly.

"Never mind," he said hastily. "Amethyst. Your will?"

"Does it really matter?" Sapphire said quietly.

"Matter!" Coral exclaimed.

Only Emerald and their father were silent, and Micah could see full well why. Emerald was scarlet, evidently shocked at the news and unable to speak…and Jasper must have known.

"Please, Micah, read it," his mother said, a slight note of pleading in her voice. "It may be important."

"More important than this?" asked Coral in wonder.

Micah swallowed. His mother was looking at him with pleading eyes, and it could not be more clear that she did not wish to discuss the intricacies of her will. Whatever had occurred between this uncle and his mother, it was painful, and…and she was ashamed.

Making restitution.

But there was no point in attempting to argue with one's mother, especially when that mother was Opal de Petras. Micah sighed and pulled apart the letter. It had no seal but was instead tied with string, which typically would have suggested it was not important at all. Anyone important would have sealed it with wax and their signet ring.

His eyes fell to the page.

Micah—I do not wish to see you again. Our arrangement is at an end. C. Tetlow

Micah blinked. No, he—he could not have read that correctly. It could not be.

He read it again. And a third time, each time the words wavering in and out of his vision, blurred, incomprehensible, for they could not mean what he thought, it was impossible.

She did not want to see him again?

"Micah?"

He ignored his mother's voice. He could ignore everything now, his entire being focused on the short note between his fingers.

She no longer wanted to see him—something had happened. Something terrible. His heart cracked, still beating but unable to sustain him. A very real pain was aching in his chest and he unconsciously put a hand to it, unable to bear it.

What had he done—what had happened to end her affection for him? Had someone said something, a damned lie, naturally, but convincing enough to persuade Catherine?

"Micah?"

Micah looked up. It was his father who had spoken, concern in his eyes.

"Micah, are you quite well?" Jasper asked quietly. "You look a little—"

"I am perfectly well," Micah snapped.

How had he managed to lose the one woman he knew he would ever love?

"N-No, I'm not," he said quietly, his gaze dropping once more to the note, in hopes that it would be altered.

It was precisely the same.

Micah—I do not wish to see you again. Our arrangement is at an end. C. Tetlow

"Micah?" That was Sapphire, speaking uncertainly.

Opal stepped forward. "Let me see it."

There was nothing in Micah to prevent it. They may as well know soon enough; he would no longer need to be given part of the shipping business. His father could keep it to himself, and Micah would disappear into his lodgings and—

"I don't understand!" Opal was all astonishment, and when Micah looked up to meet her gaze, she looked outraged. "What could you have possibly done to upset her like that?"

Sapphire sat up. "Her?"

"Her?" repeated Amethyst.

"I did not do anything," Micah said swiftly.

It had been a mistake to open it here, to betray himself—but the rush of misery had been impossible to hide. It must be painted on his face, for all the world to see.

"But she no longer wants to see you!"

"I know that," said Micah with gritted teeth.

"She? Who is this she?" said Coral, looking between her mother and brother.

"But you must have done something to—"

"I have done nothing wrong that I can recall, this is as much a shock to me as it is to you," said Micah bitterly.

What could it be? That Mr. Lister perhaps, maybe he had concocted some sort of horrible lie about Micah that was just about believable—or Lady Romeril's son, whichever one Catherine had intended to go to the opera with. Had his jealousy at being spurned made him do something to Catherine—hurt her, perhaps, if she did not break things off with Micah?

"Can someone please tell me what is going on?"

"It's nothing to do with you, Coral," Micah snapped.

Goodness, the last thing he needed was for his sister to—

"There's no need to speak to me like that," Coral said, temper flaring. "And I think anything that goes on in this family is my business, in a way, and all I asked was—"

"It's Micah's young lady," said Jasper quietly, evidently thinking it would be enough to quieten them.

Micah groaned.

"Micah's young lady?" Coral, Emerald, and Sapphire all spoke together, their eyes moving to him in a most disconcerting way.

"But Micah doesn't have a young lady!" Amethyst said, evidently lost.

"I knew it!" crowed Sapphire.

Micah sighed. "You knew nothing of the sort," he said bitterly, reaching out to his mother for the note.

She placed it back in his hand. "But—"

"Who is she?" asked Coral eagerly. "Oh, I knew you would always get married one day, Micah, it was only a matter of time before—"

"Coral," said Emerald quietly, "I do not think—"

"—and I hope I know her, I hope she is of good family and comes with a sufficient dowry," rattled on Coral, eyes bright, and Micah knew of no way to stop her. "When I think of all the young ladies in Society you might have chosen—"

"Coral," repeated Emerald. "It doesn't seem as though—"

But she continued on and on, and it did not appear any of her siblings could stop her. Micah's stomach twisted painfully as he caught Emerald's eye. She could see it. She could see the misery in his expression, the pain the note had caused.

"But she says she no longer wishes to see you again!"

Their mother's words cut Coral's monologue short, and she glared at Micah. "What did you do?"

"I did not do anything!" Micah exploded.

"You must have done something," said Amethyst.

Micah glared. *Why did she always have to get involved?*

"Perhaps it is not something you did, but something you did not do," said Sapphire archly. "Have you proposed marriage yet?"

"Sapphy!"

"All I did was ask," Sapphire said with a shrug at her mother's exclamation. "Something it appears Micah did not."

It was impossible to hide the horror on Micah's face.

"Oh, Micah, what were you waiting for?" Opal said, shaking her head wearily as though it was perfectly obvious.

"For—for everything to be sorted!" Micah stammered, pointing at his father as though that explained everything. Tight pain was overcoming his chest, but he managed to say, "You think I should have proposed before speaking to you, before ascertaining whether I even had a home to offer her?"

It was, to his complete surprise, Coral who came to his rescue. "That's a fair point, Mama. After all, everything must be aligned before—"

"It can't be that, it's been days since you came to see us, Micah," said Jasper quietly. "Are you sure there is nothing else—nothing that could have been misunderstood by the lady?"

Micah swallowed. Misunderstood by the lady? He was only starting now to appreciate just how complex and wonderful Catherine was, so it was perfectly possible he may have overstepped—*or God forbid, understepped*—at some point and not noticed.

He tried to think, the noise of the room rushing around him but fading into darkness as he closed his eyes and attempted to recall anything, everything he had done since declaring his affection.

There were only two things that came to mind. Firstly, he probably should not have asked Catherine who that lady was on the street. Surely that was not worthy of total abandonment.

And the second...

Micah's heart skipped a beat. He had not given Holland a note to put in with the one hundred pounds, the winnings of the wager they had made together. Had Catherine thought that a little heartless?

Had she hoped for...he did not know, a love letter of some kind?

"I don't know," Micah said helplessly, and the room fell silent. "I suppose I may not have been...well, as effusive as I could have been. But she—Catherine, she had never needed such things before, and she knew how I felt...I had tried to tell her, told her how she...how without her..."

His voice trailed away into misery. *What was he going to do without her?*

A gentle hand touched his shoulder, then grasped it in comfort. Micah looked up and saw, in astonishment, Coral standing by him.

"Heartbreak is never easy," she said quietly. "But you will overcome it. You are a de Petras, and you will always have your family."

"Yes," said Amethyst unexpectedly, her voice quiet. "I know what it is to feel loneliness, despair...but your sister is right. You have your family."

Micah tried to smile, but to his horror, tears started to fall down his cheeks. Yes, he had his family...but the family he had started to dare to think of with Catherine was gone. Forever.

CHAPTER EIGHTEEN

November 12, 1812

"How...how fascinating," Catherine said weakly.

There was nothing fascinating about it. In fact, she could not think of anything less fascinating, but she had asked what the gentleman's interests were, and it appeared she was paying the price.

"And the week before that, only half an inch of rain, can you believe it?" said the gentleman before her eagerly, leaning forward in his chair.

Catherine could not decide whether he did so to be close to her, or merely because he was so enthused with the topic, he simply could not help himself.

Well, each to their own, of course, and she was not the only one to typically complain a gentleman was passionate about something that laid no harm on anyone's door...

But rainfall? Truly?

"And...and when did you discover your interest in precipitation?" Catherine managed.

Lord Anthony Romeril grinned. "Oh, my word, now that is an interesting story, Miss Tetlow, I am sure you will agree, for it was when I was a young man—at least, a younger man than I am now, although I am still very young, as you can see..."

Catherine nodded politely as the words washed over her. It had been her idea. That was why she could not complain; she had been determined to ascertain before any agreement was made, whether or not the son of Lady Romeril was suitable.

Suitable, she chided silently as Lord Anthony Romeril continued talking. *Suitable!*

It was pathetic. Why, she knew—even if she would not admit it to herself—that she was very close to selecting a random man off the street and begging him to take her, if only to give her a pound.

A pound. Catherine swallowed. What she could do with a pound right now...eat something. That would be her first port of call.

Bread with dripping was not a meal, and it was all she had had in the last two days.

"—yet, of course, hail is far more difficult to measure, and yet so more unusual, it is not something I have had to contend with but eleven times since 1810, and so you can imagine my concentration has been focused on other areas, far more intriguing to..."

Catherine nodded again. That was, at least, one thing in Lord Anthony Romeril's favor. He did not appear to need any input in the conversation; something she should be grateful for.

Really...the weather? The man had no other interests?

"—show you when you come to visit me at—"

"No," interrupted Catherine swiftly.

The young man's face fell. "I...well, I thought I was doing rather well, I did not believe I had discredited myself so utterly for you to make a decision so quick—"

"I merely meant," Catherine added, trying to smile seductively as best she could, though her heart rebelled, "that I would prefer to meet here. In my rooms."

As though he could not help himself, Lord Anthony Romeril looked around the room where they were sat. Catherine tried not to. She was well aware of its rundown appearance, and certainly the son of a lord, a lord himself, would prefer far more delightful accommodation.

She cleared her throat. "I do not mean in this room in particular, you understand. I meant my…boudoir."

With a tilt of her neck, she indicated a door to their right.

Lord Anthony Romeril's expression cleared up immediately, though two red spots also appeared on his cheeks. "Oh well, if you—I mean to say, boudoir, I have never—though of course, I have had many…many encounters…"

The man's voice trailed away.

Catherine smiled wistfully. *An innocent.* Well could she remember that state, though it was a few years ago now. And so unlike—

No. She forced herself not to think of him. No good would come of the comparison, and all she would do was hurt herself in the meantime.

The fact that Lord Anthony Romeril and Micah de Petras were so different was…

She sighed, trying to rearrange her features into the same winning smile she had managed when Lord Anthony Romeril had arrived at her rooms twenty minutes before.

She would not think of him. Would not think how Micah would never have borne being interviewed in this way for the position of her lover, or how much taller he was, how much more handsome, his chiseled jaw nothing to the soft jowl of the man before her. How Micah could entertain her with almost anything—why, he could probably make rainfall interesting.

Lord Anthony Romeril was smiling. "So…so what do you think?"

Catherine's smile did not falter, but its warmth dissipated. "Think?"

Think? All she could think about was Micah.

She glanced at the door and felt the swing of her earrings.

And she should certainly put away the delightful gift he had given her. Not sell it, or give it away, just…hide it.

What from, yourself? Catherine almost snorted at her own foolishness.

She glanced at Lord Anthony Romeril, all hopeful eyes and eagerness.

She would certainly not run the same risk with him.

"I think this very promising," she said in a seductive voice, leaning forward. "Tea?"

Lord Anthony Romeril swallowed as his eyes fell to the soft swell of her décolletage—as Catherine had intended he would. "Yes, I think that would be breast—best!"

Catherine smothered a smile as she poured tea into his cup. Yes, she was almost there, had almost secured him. As long as his mother, Lady Romeril did not find out. From what Micah had said, she was an absolute tyrant!

Not that she should be thinking of Micah, of course.

"I expect you are desirous of discussing the details," Catherine said delicately.

Lord Anthony Romeril swallowed. "Yes, v-very desirous."

She tried to allow herself to feel a little pleasure at the very visible effect she was having on the young man, but it was impossible. How could one crow over seducing one man, when one's heart belonged completely to another?

"Well, we would meet once a week—"

"I-In your boudoir."

Catherine smiled. "In my boudoir, yes. It is customary, as I am sure you are aware, for a gentleman to show his…appreciation."

It was a delicate conversation this, but it had to be had. She could not simply barrel into a new arrangement without agreeing on the details.

A memory flashed through her mind; her conversation with Micah, right at the beginning of their arrangement. It had all seemed so simple—he had seemed so worldly, so wise. So impressive.

"A gentleman seeks to show his appreciation, and if we find we are

suitable, I believe my appreciation will run to...ten pounds a week."

Catherine swallowed. "I do not know whether you had any-thing in mind..."

Her voice trailed off, and her gaze caught Lord Anthony Romeril's, who swallowed himself. "I-I do not precisely know—when I asked my brother, he...thirty pounds a week?"

She managed to stop herself from gasping aloud. Thirty pounds a—thirty pounds? Why, with that money, she could send John to school, perhaps even take rooms that were suitable for both herself and Mary...assuming the girl could return to Mrs. McCall's once a week.

"I believe," said Catherine slowly, "that is highly accepta—"

But she broke off. There was the most unaccountable ruckus going on downstairs, a noise more akin to an explosion than anything she could have believed a human could create.

Lord Anthony Romeril looked round also. "What in God's name is going on?"

Catherine turned back to him hastily. She had to make this agreement, had to—how had Micah put it? Seal the deal. With a kiss. Not that she should be thinking of Micah...

"I believe we have an agreement," she said swiftly, rising to her feet. Lord Anthony Romeril mirrored her immediately. "All we need to do now is—"

The door slammed open so heavily that the one and only painting Catherine had on the wall smashed to the ground.

Lord Anthony Romeril swore, and Catherine exclaimed in surprise, but it was nothing to the shock she felt as she looked at the intruder who had so almost destroyed her chance at securing a new lover, and saw—Micah.

And not just Micah. Not the Micah she had expected. His eyes were wide, red rimmed, as though he had not slept a wink. His face was unshaven, growth grazing his jaw.

Which, Catherine tried not to notice, only made him even more handsome than before.

He was breathing heavily, as though he had run up the stairs.

"What the devil do you want, man?" Lord Anthony Romeril asked.

But Micah did not listen to him. His eyes were entirely fixed on Catherine, who felt heat rush through her chest at his intensity.

He could not be here. Perhaps she was dreaming, perhaps this entire thing was a dream. Though now she came to think about it, even she could surely not have imagined such banal conversation as rain collection...

"Get out."

For a heart-stopping moment, Catherine thought he was speaking to her. Certainly, Micah had been looking at her when he had spoken, but surely the man would not ask her to leave her own rooms?

It appeared Lord Anthony Romeril was experiencing the same confusion. "Damnit, man, the woman lives here!"

"I did not mean her," said Micah darkly, taking a further step into the room and not ceasing his stare at Catherine. "I meant you."

Catherine darted a glance at Lord Anthony Romeril, who had blushed to the intensity of a beetroot.

"You cannot be serious!"

"I have something very important to say to the lady," Micah said, stepping forward once more. "And I do not believe you will like it."

Catherine's heart was beating so fast, it was almost a whir. What was he doing here—and why was he making such a scene? What could he possibly have to say to her that could not wait until Lord Anthony Romeril departed—or better, why could he not have put it in a letter?

It was unfathomable, and it was glorious, her traitorous heart aching to be close to him, even though Catherine knew it would only mean greater heartache tomorrow.

One more kiss—one last kiss, surely she was due that...

"Micah," Catherine breathed.

"Anything you wish to say to the lady you can say before me," said Lord Anthony Romeril pompously. "I hardly think there can be anything you—"

Catherine gasped.

At least, she tried to gasp. It was rather difficult when Micah's lips were pressed hard against hers.

She clung to Micah. How he had managed to step across the room and sweep her into his arms so swiftly, she had no idea, but that did not matter. She was where she belonged now, where she wanted to be, in his strong embrace, and as her legs quivered with the intensity of the pleasure he was bestowing on her, Micah's sturdy arms held her, keeping her close.

There were words, someone was speaking, but Catherine did not care. How could she?

Micah was kissing her.

When he finally pulled away, breaking the kiss but keeping her in his arms, Catherine blinked. "Wh-What—"

"You blaggard!"

Catherine turned and saw, quite to her surprise, that Lord Anthony Romeril was still in her rooms. *Surely she had told him to go?*

"My lord, please," she began to say.

"Have you been properly interviewed?" asked Lord Anthony Romeril arrogantly, eyes bulging. "I have endured almost half an hour of—"

"Endured?" repeated Catherine, her own temper rising now.

"My lord, I have been extensively interviewed," snapped Micah, "and—"

"You cannot be offering as much money, the woman is not worth more, and—"

Catherine bristled. *The cheek!* "Hardly worth more?"

"You had better watch your mouth, my lad," Micah said with a wry chuckle, "or—"

"—and I like the lady," blustered Lord Anthony Romeril, "so I will thank you to—"

"And I love her."

The room became silent.

Catherine stared. Micah had released her now, had stepped toward Lord Anthony Romeril as though about to do him a great injury, but she could not think about that now.

"And I love her."

Had those words really come from Micah's lips? Her Micah, Micah de Petras?

Perhaps this *was* a dream. She had certainly dreamt about this moment for so long, hoped for it, even prayed for it a few times, but never had she believed after receiving that ten pounds that she would actually hear it.

But he must have said it; there was that fierce and rather furious set of his jaw that always appeared when he said something bold.

It appeared Lord Anthony Romeril had heard him too. "You what?"

"Get out."

Catherine blanched. She had wondered for a moment who had said those words, only to find she had.

Lord Anthony Romeril's eyes bulged. "I beg your pardon?"

"I mean, I need to discuss something with Mr. de Petras that is most urgent," said Catherine in a rush, stepping toward the interloper and pulling him, none too gently, to the open door. "I will send you a note with my—"

"But I have told you all about my rain—"

"And very interesting it was, too," she said firmly, heart in her mouth, desperate to get rid of the man. "Goodbye, my lord."

Catherine slammed the door behind him and leaned against it, lifting her eyes slowly to meet the gaze of Micah de Petras.

He was glaring. "You considered that oaf?"

"I needed him," breathed Catherine, hardly sure why they were talking about Lord Anthony Romeril when Micah had just announced his love for her. "But I don't want to be treated like a mistress anymore."

Did he understand? Could he see in her eyes, hear in her voice what she meant?

Micah closed the gap between them but still kept a few paces back, as though she could scald him if he got too close. "I know."

"Do you?" challenged Catherine, her voice breaking. "Do you, Micah? Because I thought I knew, and you knew what we meant to each other, and you—"

"I thought so, too!" Micah interjected, and there was pain in his voice, though Catherine could not understand why. "I thought by sending you that money—"

She could not help but laugh, a painful laugh that was an echo of the pain in her heart. "You think treating me like the mistress I always had been was a demonstration of your affection?"

The confusion that covered Micah's expression was mystifying. "Demonstration of—treating you like the mistress...Catherine, I paid you the winnings of the wager!"

"If I succeed, which I will, then you...you will give me one hundred pounds."

Catherine swallowed. No, that was not right. She could clearly remember taking out a ten-pound note, and there was nothing else in that letter save the note written by someone other than Micah.

"You...you sent me ten pounds," she breathed, holding onto the doorknob for support. "What was I supposed to think?"

For a moment, absolute confusion hung in the air. How could they have so dreadfully misunderstood each other?

Micah hung his head, shaking it with a wry laugh. "Oh, dear God. Holland."

"Holland?"

"My manservant—the manservant, I suppose, for my lodgings."

Catherine stared. "I thought I knew him from somewhere!"

"I told him," said Micah heavily, "to send you one hundred pounds. I was very clear on that, one hundred pounds, the result of our wager. The wager for my heart which I could not help but admit you had won."

Her pulse was roaring so loudly in her ears that Catherine was not sure whether she had heard him correctly, but there was such contrition on his face, such shame…

"You…you told him to bring me one hundred pounds," she breathed.

Micah nodded, a shy smile teasing his lips. "One hundred pounds. I mean, the moment I realized I was completely in love with you—"

"You are in love with me."

Catherine could not help but repeat it. Hearing it again and again, she could not hear it enough. So strong, yet so fragile, this love of theirs. Too easily broken.

"I am in love with you," said Micah softly, raising his hand and grazing her cheek with his fingers. "I have, despite what I so foolishly thought, fallen completely in love with you. Painfully so, actually, it actually hurts to be away from—anyway. I don't want anyone else, Cat, I want you. Only you."

"I knew you would fall in love with me," Catherine said shakily, hardly able to believe it. "I knew if you just considered me for a moment—"

"And you were right." Micah laughed dryly. "Far more right than I could have predicted. Damnit, Cat, seeing you there with that man—"

"Lord Anthony Romeril."

"I know the man's name, I stayed with him as a child for a few days when my father…it doesn't matter." Micah drew a hand distractedly through his hair. "The point is, I am in love with you, and you don't have to look for any other man."

Catherine could hardly believe it, but as she nodded, a rush of joy burst her heart open. "I did not want to be Lord Anthony Romeril's mistress."

"I know."

"I don't want to be your mistress either."

"I know."

"But I had to—I must protect my family, Micah," Catherine said in a faltering voice. *She had to make him understand, she did not come alone.* "My brother and sister, I must—"

"I know," Micah said softly, stepping forward so that he was but a few inches away.

Catherine swallowed. "I-I am so in love with you, Micah."

It felt strange, finally saying it aloud.

Micah chuckled. "I know."

"And you—you love me?" Catherine blinked.

"You are a very determined mistress, Catherine Tetlow," said Micah quietly, his blazing eyes fixed fiercely on hers, "and that is one of the reasons I have fallen in love with you. You know what you want, and you don't stop until you get it."

It was hard to argue with such a statement. "I suppose, in a way, that is true."

They loved each other. *They loved each other?* Catherine could hardly believe it, hardly believe they had finally reached an understanding that she had craved for so long.

And now she craved him, all of him. It was a sweet torture to have him so close and yet not be touching him. Why, if he only leaned a little closer.

"So, you'll marry me then?"

Catherine stared. "What?"

Was that how it happened? Was that how perfect happiness was reached, with such a matter-of-fact statement given by a gentleman who was at any moment going to kiss her, she could see it in his eyes—as though it was a perfectly natural thing to say?

"Yes," Catherine breathed, reaching out her fingers to grasp Micah's lapels and pull him closer, her lips brushing his own just the once before she allowed him to capture her mouth with his.

CHAPTER NINETEEN

November 30, 1812

"ABSOLUTELY NOT," SAID Micah with a dry laugh. "No, I forbid it!"

"You can't forbid it!" said the delicate blonde lying in his arms.

Micah breathed in the scent of Catherine and knew he would never be able to live without her. Which was no longer his concern; not now she had promised to be his wife, their wedding just a week away.

Which was why it was so vital that they finally agreed on the last remaining decision that lay before them.

He had not considered it complicated. After all, there was only one obvious solution, and if Catherine could let him get a word in edgewise, he could explain it to her.

As it was…

"I just think my rooms are better placed in town than yours," Catherine said firmly as she twisted in his arms, propping herself up on an elbow. "I am far closer to your family—"

"That is not necessarily a benefit," Micah said wryly.

"—and close to the best part of town for patisseries—"

"That is a benefit."

"—and besides, my rooms are far cheaper than yours," Catherine pointed out.

Micah almost moaned at the sensation of his future bride pressed against him like that. They had promised each other, hadn't they, not to indulge in lovemaking until the wedding.

Keep something special for our wedding night, that was how Catherine had put it. Micah had called it a special kind of torture.

It was getting ridiculous. Here they were, lying on the bed fully clothed, and his manhood was still standing at attention. And after all, Micah had tried to convince Catherine only last week, there were plenty of things he could do to her, things they could share…

"So, we're decided. We'll live in my rooms," said Catherine decidedly.

"Absolutely not," repeated Micah with a laugh. "Catherine, your rooms are dire!"

"Micah!"

"I am sorry to say it, but I cannot help the truth," he countered with a grin. "Even you must admit you only took them because they were the most economical you could find at the time."

Catherine had no need to speak; he could see the truth in her eyes. "That is a coincidence."

"I am not going to live in your rooms," said Micah firmly.

"Well, we can't live here!"

Now that was a surprise to him. He had not expected Catherine to be so certain of that. Micah blinked, then looked around his bedchamber.

It was a decent size, well apportioned with a pleasant aspect from the window. The adjoining rooms were in far better repair than Catherine's, and he had a manservant.

Well. The building had a manservant, but they could use him.

"I have no idea why not, and you have no reasons other than pique," he said.

Catherine raised an eyebrow. "You cannot think of a single reason why I may not wish to live here?"

Micah swallowed. He thought of Polly, who had visited three times; Annie, who had only one room of her own and so had frequently come here; and that courtesan he had once…

He sighed heavily. "Well, perhaps there is one reason."

"You mean you have had other mistresses here?"

Micah smiled weakly. It was not something he was ashamed of. Not exactly. After all, he could hardly have known he was going to meet Catherine beforehand, and he had even less knowledge that one day he would fall in love with her and wish to make her his wife.

How many men married their mistresses?

"You mean you wish to find somewhere in London where I haven't bedded a woman?" he asked archly.

Catherine flicked him on the nose. "I'll do it again."

Micah rubbed at his nose. "I am not saying there is no-where—no!"

He pushed her hand away as they both fell into laughter, twisting on the bed until Catherine was lying beside him. Micah turned onto his side and grinned at the beautiful woman beside him.

How could he ever have considered her purely a mistress? How had it managed to get it into his head that he did not care for this woman, adore her?

Catherine Tetlow, anyone else's woman? Anyone else's wife—no.

"Will we have to move to another town to escape all the women you have bedded?"

"I knew there was a reason I wanted to marry you," Micah teased.

She laughed with him. Surely no other man had such a winsome wife, a woman who could laugh at his mistakes just as much as he could.

Catherine was perfect. She was everything.

"I was the one who wanted to marry you," she corrected him.

"And you should have said something sooner," Micah said in a mock angry voice, "for we could have had so much more time…"

His voice trailed away as the thought echoed in his mind.

To think Catherine could have been his wife for a year, perhaps more! That he could have woken up every morning to her soft welcoming arms, her kisses, spend all day in her company, hear her laughter, have the honor of making her laugh…

And every night, enjoy her lovemaking.

Micah smiled. Why wait until the night? When she was his wife, and he was finally able to show her, not just tell her how much he desired her, there would not be an hour when he would not—

"I did say something sooner."

Micah blinked. "You did?"

"Oh, not with words, exactly," said Catherine with a rueful smile.

Oh, she was incredible.

"Well, looking for lodgings sounds like a hopeless business," he said with a shrug. "I do declare, even if we combed the entirety of London, we would not find somewhere sufficient for us."

There was just a hint of concern now in Catherine's brows. "You…you don't think we'll find anywhere to rent?"

Micah shook his head.

"But we marry in less than a week!"

"We do," groaned Micah, "a length of time growing longer with each passing—"

"Micah!"

Micah grinned. "What?"

Catherine looked rather pointedly at his hand which had somehow managed to find itself a warm home on her hip. "We agreed."

"I did not know what I was agreeing to," Micah groaned. "Staying away, it is—"

"You're hardly staying away."

He smiled.

"We need to find somewhere to live, if we are agreed neither of our lodgings are suitable," pointed out Catherine.

There was just a hint of concern in her voice.

She would make a marvelous mistress of a home. It had already made her a rather spectacular mistress.

"In that case, I think you will be delighted to hear I have found the perfect place," he announced.

His heart had twisted as he said the words. Would she agree? Had he been too forceful, charging ahead without her?

The opportunity to surprise her had been too great, he had not been able to help himself—but as Micah glanced at Catherine, he saw far more concern there than he had wanted.

Had he perhaps gone too far?

"You have?" asked Catherine, raising an eyebrow.

Micah nodded, joy in his heart. *Oh, the anticipation was almost too much!* "I have."

"Without consulting me?" asked Catherine, pushing herself up on her elbows.

For just a fraction of a hesitation, Micah swallowed. He knew better than any man in London just how much a woman liked to be involved in decision-making. After all, had he not been raised in a house where his mother had, for several years, been the only parent?

Even now, after his father had returned, it was Opal de Petras and not Jasper who had the final say on decisions.

"I have not taken it," he said hastily.

Catherine lowered herself. "Oh. I see. You have just seen it?"

Micah thought back to the viewing the day before. He had not thought to invite Catherine, had wanted it to be a surprise. Only now did he wonder whether that was, perhaps, not precisely the best way to go about things.

"I have seen it," he said evasively. "It truly is a lovely home, Catherine, you would indeed approve of it, and it only went up for sale—"

"For sale?" Catherine sat up completely now, eyes wide. "Micah, are you mad? With the allowance your mother gives you—"

"Oh, I knew there was something I had forgotten to tell you," said Micah triumphantly, as though he had carefully concocted this entire conversation precisely for this revelation when he had in fact merely stumbled through it. "I no longer have an allowance."

Catherine's eyes widened, if possible, even more. "No allowance?"

Micah grinned. *Oh, she was going to be so happy when she—*

"No allowance? Micah, do we need to—I hate to suggest it," said Catherine frantically, "but if postponing the wedding will give us time to—"

"I no longer have an allowance because I have an income."

Catherine stared as Micah's whole chest swelled with pride. Was this what it was to truly surprise one's wife? Not wife, but it was only a week, and she would be his. All his...

"An income," Catherine repeated.

Micah nodded. "It was why I was so late to...well, why I did not propose matrimony immediately. My father's shipping business, you see, he always said that he would make me a partner, sign over part of the business to me."

She was still staring. Micah had thought it a reasonable explanation, but evidently more was required.

"You see," he continued, "my mother has the wealth and fortune, but it is my father's shipping business—he started it himself before my parents were married, and when he was misplaced for seven years—"

"Misplaced? For seven years?"

"Not important, "said Micah hastily. That was a story best told in full, and he had far more interesting things to discuss. "The important thing is, two days ago my father and I completed the paperwork at Parker, Bells, and Hamble. I now have an income."

Catherine was blinking as though he had just announced he was the prince of a distant country. "Are...are you in earnest?"

Micah smiled nervously. "I am. To the tune of fifteen hundred a year."

He had spoken proudly; had been astonished to hear his father wished to sign over not half, but three-quarters of the shipping business he had worked so hard to build.

And fifteen hundred a year...why, it was near double the allowance given by his mother, and he knew for a fact it was almost three times the amount Catherine had lived on. It was a generous offer, and it would permit them to live in a style Micah was ready to become accustomed to.

But Catherine did not appear to be so impressed. Her eyes had not calmed, her mouth had fallen open, and there was an ashen color to her expression Micah did not like.

"Cat?" he said quietly. "Catherine? I-I thought it would be—if you wish it to be more, I suppose there is—"

"More?" Catherine interrupted, breathing the word. "More? More than fifteen hundred a—fifteen hundred a year?"

All the tension melted away from Micah's shoulders. "You are not—I thought for a moment there you were disappointed."

"Disappointed?" Catherine laughed, her eyes still wide but her lips curling into a smile. "Micah, we are rich!"

"We are indeed."

"And we can buy a house!"

"The one I saw yesterday I think would be perfect for us," Micah said eagerly. "Honestly, Catherine, I think it is flawless."

She laughed as she raised an eyebrow. "And precisely how close is it to your club?"

"Not in the slightest," Micah laughed.

"It is in a respectable part of town," Micah said grinning. "A full townhouse, not simply a floor with a few rooms."

Catherine swallowed. "Truly?"

His gaze drifted to the earrings in Catherine's ears. His earrings, the ones he had given her as a thank you. He had never felt such vibrant delight at giving anything before. But this was different. This was more.

There was still so much to tell her…

"Truly, I think we should buy it," Micah said. "A large drawing room, facing the mid-afternoon sun, and a dining room—"

"A dining room?"

"And sufficient kitchens for a maid, a cook, and a manservant," continued Micah eagerly, details spilling from his lips now he had finally permitted himself to speak of it. "And eight bedchambers!"

For some reason, Catherine did not look delighted at this piece of news. "Eight?"

Micah nodded gleefully. *Oh, couldn't she see?* Perhaps she could not, but that would make the revelation all the sweeter.

There was a strange sort of stirring in his chest, right by his heart, that he had never felt before. It was akin to joy but deeper than that. Something about being a part of Catherine, planning a life together…it gave him this overwhelming sense of peace.

"Eight?" repeated Catherine. "Micah de Petras, what are we going to do with eight bedchambers?"

"Well," he said, excitement roaring through him, "your siblings are coming to live with us, for a start."

It did not appear that Catherine had understood him. That, or she had misunderstood him. She merely looked at him, expressionless, as though he had said nothing.

"Are…are you…my siblings? John and Mary?"

Micah nodded. "Of course. They are family, Catherine, and though I may not always be on the right side of mine, there is nothing more important than family."

And then she rushed to pull him into an embrace, a tight one that had nothing to do with lovemaking and everything to do with affection, and Micah clung to her, desperately happy he had done something so right.

"Oh, Micah, I-I had not wanted to ask, but—both of them?"

"Both of them," he reassured her.

Catherine kissed him. "We'll all be together again!"

"After too long," Micah said, his arms around the woman he loved. "Honestly, I do not think I could have lived with myself if we did not have them."

How long they were on the bed, embracing tightly, Micah did not know. He had learned not to count such moments; they were going to continue on forever, after all, every day filled with them like sparkling sunlight.

"Well," she said eventually, pulling away and half sighing, half laughing as she leaned against the headboard. "I suppose that accounts for four of the bedchambers."

A small frown creased Micah's forehead. "Four?"

Catherine nodded.

Confusion trickled into his mind. *Four?* One for them, for they had not the habits of the aristocracy to do something as wild as have separate but adjoining bedchambers...one for John, one for Mary...could she mean Sapphire?

Micah loved his sister, he even liked her, which was saying something, but he had absolutely no intention of the girl living with them!

"I don't understand," he confessed finally, spotting the dancing smile on Catherine's lips but not comprehending it. "Ours, your brother's, and your sister's...but who else joins us?"

Catherine did nothing but smile.

"Do not try to tell me that Lord Anthony Romeril—"

She flicked him on the nose again. "Don't be silly!"

"Well, who then?" Micah was at a loss. He could not think of anyone who would—

"Our baby."

It was his turn to blink in astonishment this time. Micah stared, unable to comprehend what he had just heard. Their...baby. Their baby?

"Baby," he repeated, as though that would make the word more real.

More real? How much more real could a baby be? But Micah could not take it in, could not understand why Catherine was saying such a thing, unless…

His gaze sharpened. They were sitting on the bed, yes, but Catherine's hands had rather naturally fallen to her stomach. Curving around it.

He swallowed. *Baby.*

"Baby?" he repeated again, this time more weakly.

Catherine's gaze did not falter as she nodded silently.

"Oh, Cat," he breathed as he pulled her once again into his arms.

Catherine was warm and wonderful, and Micah could not believe he was so fortunate. A family of their own—just the start, surely!

"You are happy?"

"Happy?" Micah pulled away and grinned, happiness spilling out into his words. "I was shocked when you first said that you—a baby!"

"A baby," Catherine said sagely with a smile.

"But we've been so careful, we have never before—"

"Until now," she said, laughing. "And just in time, don't you think? Now I am no longer your mistress, and am about to become your wife?"

His wife. His baby. Micah could not stand it any longer, he had to express just how wonderful this news was.

He placed a delicate kiss on Catherine's lips, but he wasn't finished there. Shifting down the bed, Micah kissed, very gently, Catherine's stomach.

"My mistress, my wife, my baby," breathed Micah, hardly knowing how he would survive this happiness. "A little de Petras. Oh, Catherine…"

EPILOGUE

January 14, 1813

S *APPHIRE…*

"I still cannot believe," said Coral darkly, "we are here."

Sapphire glanced at her oldest sister—the almost eleven-year age difference only seeming to increase the more motherly Coral became—and sighed happily. "Really? I thought we always would."

They had arrived at Micah and Catherine's new home at the same time and so had entered together. Received the tour together.

Really, Sapphire was all agog at the idea of Micah living in an actual house. She had been young when he had left home—how old? She could not recall—and she had only been permitted to visit his lodgings once. Mama had refused ever since.

But this…this was a real home.

"—and the drawing room, more than big enough for family gatherings, of which I hope you will favor us," the newest Mrs. de Petras said a little breathlessly.

Sapphire beamed. "We would be honored—won't we, Coral?"

"What?" Coral blinked at the pair of them as Sapphire saw, out of the corner of her eye, Micah rolling his eyes. "Oh yes, very pleasant, I am sure. But do you not wonder whether this part of London, the expense of stabling a horse here—"

"No one wants to hear about your money quibbles here, Coral," Micah snapped.

Sapphire swallowed. *Had they ever, truly, been friends?*

Brothers and sisters were, she knew, not automatically designed to be close. Indeed, whenever she met with Lady Rose Romeril, the woman could not stop complaining about her two brothers—though, in truth, it sounded like she had more than enough cause to.

But Micah and Coral were so similar, that was what was so strange, to Sapphire's mind. Two people, two siblings with enough boldness and brashness for several. The same passion, the same eagerness to be the center of attention—

"—and I had not considered how many servants you will keep, why, wages alone—"

"I did not ask you, Coral!"

Sapphire stepped closer to her new sister-in-law. "They are always like this. Don't let it worry you."

"I know," said Catherine de Petras softly. "And I don't. Micah has told me enough about Coral for me to be certain there is always blame on both sides."

Sapphire was impressed. Here was a woman they had never met, never heard of until a few months ago, and she had already sized up her siblings rather magnificently.

But then she recollected herself, her cheeks staining with heat.

Of course. Catherine had been Micah's mistress—for how long, her brother had refused to say. All that was important now, he had said tersely the only time their mother had asked, was that she was his wife.

And Sapphire was inclined to agree. Oh, it was mortifying to think of her brother—but then, Catherine was so pleasant. A fine addition to the family.

"—and while I don't forget—"

"Ah, here you all are," came a new voice.

Sapphire turned with relief to see the final de Petras sibling enter the room—hesitantly, of course, as was her way, but with the reassurance of her husband and child behind her.

"Emerald!"

"Your ladyship," came the quiet welcome of their hostess.

Sapphire snorted. "You don't have to call her that! We're not going to start calling Coral Your Grace, after all."

She saw her eldest sister's cheeks flush. "Well, it would not do you any harm if—"

"You found the place fine, then?" Sapphire said, pushing past Coral's nonsense and beaming at her niece. "Hullo, Beryl. What have you got there?"

Emerald's little one hid behind her father's legs only for a moment before bounding out and proudly presenting the doll she was holding.

"Amber," she said proudly.

Sapphire beamed at the little girl. "So I see. May I look at her?"

Beryl nodded, holding out the doll. "Can you hold her, without a hand?"

The question did not even cause Sapphire's heart to skip a beat. "Of course I can! Look."

She carefully took the doll from her niece's hands, then showed her how she could, with the delicate use of her stub, remove the little gown on the toy, then place it back on.

"See?"

Beryl nodded. "Mine now."

Without another word, the little girl took the doll back from Sapphire and scampered off to show another one of her relatives.

Sapphire straightened up with a wry smile. There were always going to be questions, she knew. There always had been, no matter what stage of life she had been in. Questions she did not mind, as long as they were asked in genuine curiosity, an eagerness to learn, a desire to treat her just as any other woman.

Children never bothered her. It was the adults which made

her life so…

Sapphire swallowed. She would not think of it—there were so few people who treated her as a strange thing to look at, rather than the woman she was. Besides, she was with family.

"My word, look at your doll!" Catherine had cried with genuine interest, lowering herself onto her haunches to look her new niece in the eyes. "And does she have a name?"

Sapphire smiled. It was pleasant to see the newest member of the family fit in so well. Really, she must make sure to remember to congratulate Micah at some point. He truly had managed to find a wife who was outstanding: pleasant, pretty, and entirely at ease with the family.

"And what is her favorite thing to do?" Catherine continued softly as the little girl rabbited on before her.

Sapphire sighed heavily. It was remarkably pleasant, after years of being the youngest in the family, to have new ones to shower with adoration. After all, she had always hated being called—

"Little one! I did not know you were here, we would have taken you in the carriage," came the warm tones of her mother.

Sapphire tried to keep her face calm as she turned to her parents. "Don't call me that."

"Don't call you what?" asked Opal breezily, kissing Emerald on the cheek and walking toward her hostess. "My dear…"

"I always hated being called that, too," said Coral unexpectedly.

"And me," said Emerald with a laugh. "But I was not called it for long."

"You were all called little one?" Amethyst frowned slightly. "But surely Sapphire is the youngest?"

Sapphire scowled. Why, it was most infuriating. There were eight years between her and Emerald, but it may as well have been twenty years, for all the fuss they had made of her.

In truth, not that she would ever admit it to anyone, she had enjoyed it when truly little. It was nice to be the baby of the family, to always get one's own way, to be forgiven quicker and believed immediately.

But the way they still treated her—

"Hello, little one," said her father, beaming.

Sapphire sighed. "Papa—"

"I know, I know," said Jasper, raising his hands in surrender. "You don't like it."

"It's not that I don't—"

"Edward not joining us?" asked Robert breezily, stepping past Emerald, his wife, to shake hands with Micah. "I thought we'd all be here."

"This isn't actually a formal gathering," said Micah, glancing at his wife.

Sapphire watched, curious. It was all very strange, these marriages. Oh, she liked her new sister-in-law and both of her brothers-in-law. *Thank goodness.* Lord, she had no idea what she would have done if she had believed them cads, or worse, rakes, unworthy to be married to anyone let alone her sisters.

But they were pleasant sorts of chaps, as gentlemen went, and Sapphire found it fascinating how their appearance in the family had changed things. Changed her siblings. Not softened them exactly…well, perhaps in Micah's case. He had even attended the family dinner last Saturday, which was a marvel to behold.

But there was something different about the way a husband and wife spoke to each other. Sapphire had first noticed it when Coral and Edward had wed, and then she had started noticing it in their parents. Now she was surrounded by them; wedded couples, that was.

If only she—

"Come, little one, sit by the fire," called her mother from across the room. "You'll catch a chill!"

"Mama, these rooms are plenty warm enough," said Micah, again looking nervously at Catherine.

Sapphire glanced at her hostess, too, and saw all the tell-tale signs of nerves that she more often associated with Emerald. Of course, she had to remember that Micah's wife still, apparently, felt as though she had to impress them.

Impress them? The de Petrases?

They had more scandal pouring out of their ears than they knew what to do with.

"Well, I must say how pleasant it is for us all to be together," said Jasper happily.

Sapphire blinked. Micah and Catherine's drawing room certainly felt very full, almost every seat taken—only two of the family were missing.

"Where is Edward?" asked Opal.

Coral sighed heavily as she sat down in an armchair. "He had to visit the estates again—it's very irritating, we were only there at Christmas, and having him so far away—"

"—going perfectly," came a quiet whisper only Sapphire seemed to notice. She turned ever so slightly and saw her brother placing a kiss on his new wife's forehead. "Everyone is having a wonderful time."

"But they don't know—"

"They love you," said Micah softly, and Sapphire was almost embarrassed to see this moment of intense affection between the newlyweds. "And why wouldn't they? If they learn to love you half as much as I love you, then you will be adored indeed."

Sapphire watched the nervous smile on Catherine's face but hurriedly looked away as they approached the rest of the family.

"And what about your siblings, Catherine?" Emerald asked quietly, smiling encouragingly. "I suppose they are at school."

"They are, yes," said Catherine, returning the smile with a shy one of her own. "I am so grateful to Micah for sending them to—"

"They are my brother and sister-in-law now, I suppose," said Micah with a dry laugh. "I have to admit, I presumed they would be older, but it is an honor to send them to school. Little John will end up better educated than me!"

"Mary, too, probably," said Robert.

The whole family laughed, Sapphire with them. Oh, this was wonderful; she loved the hustle and bustle of a family setting, all of them together—well, almost all of them—enjoying the—

"Well, I am afraid it will be difficult for me to think of them as the little ones," said Opal with a laugh. "That will always be Sapphire!"

The laughter that rang out this time was not quite so welcome to Sapphire.

She scowled. "I am not—"

"I would never think of you as little one," said Amethyst, and Sapphire was astonished to see her cousin attempting a joke, of all things. "Not in front of your face, anyway!"

"I am not the little one!"

"Saying it does not make it true," cut in Micah with a laugh. "Come on, Sapphy, we all held you as a baby! You cannot blame us for thinking of you as the little one still."

"In fairness, I did not," said Robert quietly.

Sapphire cast a grateful look at Emerald's husband. *Really, it was most infuriating!* What did a woman have to do in this family to be taken seriously?

"And such a beautiful baby she was," Jasper was saying. "I do not mean that little Amber is not delightful, Coral—"

"Having held both babies, I would argue that my Amber is more delightful," said Coral with a laugh. "But I suppose there is a certain level of bias."

There were gentle chuckles from the other mothers in the room. Sapphire glanced at Catherine and saw to her surprise that she was flushing.

Now that was interesting…

"Am I a little one?"

Sapphire beamed at the question from Beryl. "Yes, that—"

"No, that is Aunt Sapphire's special name," said Emerald with a smile that, if it was on the face of anyone else, Sapphire would have said was mischievous. "Her special family name."

Sapphire groaned, but this only seemed to elicit even more chuckles.

"It's not so bad, is it?" Robert said bracingly. "I can think of worse."

"I am still Catty to my siblings," said Catherine with a warm smile. "No matter what I say to the contrary."

"But that is at least close to your own name," Sapphire pointed out, sitting heavily on the end of the sofa. "I am near eighteen years of age!"

"And you will always be my littlest one," her father said gently. "Which reminds me, whose turn is it to accompany Sapphire to her next invitation?"

Sapphire groaned again. "I do not need a chaperone—"

"I did it last," said Coral quickly. "And with Amber growing so quickly, I could not possibly—"

"Do I count?" asked Amethyst with a grin. "I suppose I need a chaperone of my own, really."

"We'll do it," said Micah with a laugh. "I have missed out on so many, it is only fair that I—"

Sapphire's blood was boiling. "I do not need a chaperone. I am more than old enough to go myself!"

Really, it was outrageous! Coral was out in Society by this age, attending balls and dinners and card parties and all sorts of things on her own! Emerald...well, Emerald hated going out, so Sapphire had to admit that she was not a particularly good comparison.

But Micah had been sneaking out of the de Petras home and going here, there, and everywhere since he was seventeen!

Sapphire slumped against the sofa as the conversation washed over her, as her family tried to agree who was going to, in effect, be babysitting her.

It was outrageous!

One day, Sapphire vowed to herself, and one day soon, she would do something. Something...impressive. Something dramatic.

Something that would make the whole de Petras family sit up and take notice.

Discover precisely how Sapphire is going to shock her family—and the consequences of her decision—in The Convenient Engagement...Book 5 of THE DE PETRAS SAGA.

About Emily E K Murdoch

If you love falling in love, then you've come to the right place.

I am a historian and writer and have a varied career to date: from examining medieval manuscripts to designing museum exhibitions, to working as a researcher for the BBC to working for the National Trust.

My books range from England 1050 to Texas 1848, and I can't wait for you to fall in love with my heroes and heroines!

Follow me on twitter and instagram @emilyekmurdoch, find me on facebook at facebook.com/theemilyekmurdoch, and read my blog at www.emilyekmurdoch.com.